The Tumbling MIRTH

Remembering the
Air Force

The
Tumbling
MIRTH

Remembering the
Air Force

J. DOUGLAS HARVEY

McClelland and Stewart

The Canadian Publishers
McClelland and Stewart Limited
25 Hollinger Road
Toronto, M4B 3G2

Canadian Cataloguing in Publication Data

Harvey, J. Douglas, 1922-
  The tumbling mirth

ISBN 0-7710-4038-5

1. Harvey, J. Douglas, 1922-   2. Canada. Royal
Canadian Air Force – Biography.   3. Canada. Royal
Canadian Air Force – Anecdotes, facetiae, satire, etc.
I. Title.

UG626.H37   358.4'00971   C83-098607-3

Printed and bound in Canada by Gagne Ltd.

For Elizabeth Jane

Contents

Introduction / *ix*

Wild Blue Yonder / *11*

Cough and Go Aircrew / *19*

Circuits and Bumps / *33*

Celestial Bodies / *45*

Dinner at Seven / *59*

People Are Special / *73*

Per Ardua Ad Astra / *93*

How to Bend Them / *113*

For You the War is Over / *127*

Fall Out the Officers / *139*

The Paper War / *153*

VIP's / *165*

Shatterproof and Prune / *179*

Testing, Testing / *191*

Around the World / *205*

Vive la France! / *219*

Northern Lights / *233*

The Nature of Things / *249*

Introduction

Once there was an air force.

It was called by various names during its embryonic years until on April 1, 1924, it was blessed by the Governor General and became the Royal Canadian Air Force, (RCAF). On April 1, 1984, it would have celebrated its sixtieth birthday. But something happened along the way, and it disappeared in 1967 in a cloud of governmental euphoria called unification.

Gone were the Battle Honours, the Ensign, the Colours, the Badges, the Ranks, the Uniforms, and the Motto – *Per Ardua Ad Astra*. They were swept away with all the other hard-won symbols in one singularly stupid government act. Canadians were to forget that the RCAF ever existed; that it was the fourth largest air force in the world during the Second World War; that its exploits matched or exceeded those of any air force.

O, Canada.

This book is an attempt to recall, through yarns and anecdotes, some of the courage and humour that was the very fibre of the RCAF. It is a record of some of those heroic and hilarious moments that were so much a part of service in that grand organization.

You will be pleased to find that not all the stories are mine. Many people from all parts of Canada were good enough to talk to me or to send me anecdotes that they had cherished for years. I enjoyed writing them into the book, for they kept me laughing and remembering – and it is obvious from some of the tales that I'm not the only one who misses those far-off days. The anecdotes cover a long period of time: from the First World War to the present. They concern events that happened in almost every part of the world.

If this collection is anything, it is one man's effort to provide a very human memorial of the RCAF by bringing together a sample of some of the things that were done and said in the air and on the ground, in war and in peace. In asking those who served in the RCAF – or who were allied with it in some capacity – to send in their favourite anecdotes, I was asking for recognition of the crazy humour that, for all of us, was part of life in the RCAF. These are the people you should thank, and the ones I would like to salute:

Pamela E. Anderson, Russ Armstrong, Norm Avery, Bruce Beatty, Dan Brennan, Harry Bryant, Ron Butcher, C.A. Chartier, Guy Chevrette, W.H. "Butch" Cleaver, R.M. Culbert, Norman Emmott, Bill Hooper, M.I. Horton, Eric Hurd, Rosemary Hutchinson, Len Lapeer, Peter S. Lennie, J.D. Long, J.D. Loukes, Jim Lovelace, John Mahoney, Don McKechnie, John Miskae, Jessie Nason, Eric Nichol, Paul Nyznik, George Penfold, Everett Richards, A.J. Snow, Eric Stofer, D.H. Thorne, N.R. Timmerman, Derek Todd, C.L. Toomer, Rocky Van Vliet, Chester Wallace, Thomas E. Whitehouse, Thomas Wilby, Maurice V. Winton, Roy Wood.

I toyed with the idea of including a large section of photographs in this book, but decided, instead, to scatter cartoons throughout. The cartoons are mostly those drawn by Warrant Officer Ray Tracy, who will be forever remembered for bringing Sergeant Shatterproof to life. A few of the yarns, in slightly different form, have appeared in three magazines: *The Roundel*, *Legion*, and *Airforce*. I wish to thank the publishers and editors for their permission to use these pieces.

J.D.H.

Wild Blue Yonder

There have been many poems, odes, verses, and sonnets written about the air force. Some are good, some are bad, but they all have one thing in common: they attempt to define that mystic combination of youth and aviation – the feeling it brings that is so evasive of definition.

My favourite aviation poem over the years has been "High Flight," by John Gillespie Magee, Junior. Widely-known, it was the official poem of the air force, and it is still being published.

Magee was born in Shanghai, China, where his parents were American missionaries. He came to Canada to enlist in the RCAF in 1940; and a year later, he was a Spitfire pilot with the RCAF's 412 fighter squadron in Britain. He was killed in December, 1941, when he was only nineteen.

Magee had taken a high-level flying course at RAF Farnborough, and it was there he got the inspiration for his poem. He scribbled the lines on the back of a letter he sent to his mother:

Oh, I have slipped the surly bonds of earth
And danced the skies on laughter-silvered wings;
Sunward I've climbed and joined the tumbling mirth
Of sun-split clouds – and done a hundred things
You have not dreamed of – wheeled and soared and swung
High in the sunlit silence. Hov'ring there,
I've chased the shouting wind along and flung
My eager craft through footless halls of air.
Up, up the long delirious, burning blue
I've topped the wind-swept heights with easy grace,
Where never lark, or even eagle, flew;
And, while with silent, lifting mind I've trod
The high untrespassed sanctity of space,
Put out my hand and touched the face of God.

To me, "High Flight" will always represent those first days of youthful adventure when, alone in your aircraft and freed from nagging discipline, you challenged the sky.

Tom Farley, late of the National Film Board, wrote many well-received poems of air force days. Farley's poetry directed itself more to the hard details of flying operations, and his style can evoke very poignant memories. One poem he wrote, called "Dawn Sweep," has a three line closing stanza that succinctly summarizes every fighter pilot's moment of truth:

> *O did you wake*
> *Big as forever in the split snap-second*
> *That lies between the firing and the break?*

An "air force" poem that was written long before there was an air force anywhere in the world has always been a favourite of mine. "Oft in the Stilly Night," by Thomas Moore is, of course, an English classic. I think it could well represent the feelings of all the aircrews in all the wars, who are alive today:

> *Oft, in the stilly night,*
> *Ere Slumber's chain has bound me,*
> *Fond Memory brings the light*
> *Of other days around me;*
> *The smiles, the tears,*
> *Of boyhood's years ...*
>
> ...
>
> *When I remember all*
> *The friends, so linked together,*
> *I've seen around me fall,*
> *Like leaves in wintry weather;*
> *I feel like one*
> *Who treads alone*
> *Some banquet-hall deserted,*
> *Whose lights are fled,*
> *Whose garlands dead,*
> *And all but he departed!*

*   *   *

Then there's the letter that was written to the *Glasgow Herald*. It sums up what most of us know about operating in space: "In view of the great expense and difficulty in firing rockets at the moon, attempts should be made when the moon is full. There would be a better chance of hitting this full target than of hitting the thin crescent."

*   *   *

Have you ever wondered about the origin of the roundel? It came into being from pure necessity. In the opening weeks of the First World War, any aircraft flying over the lines could expect a volley of rifle fire from

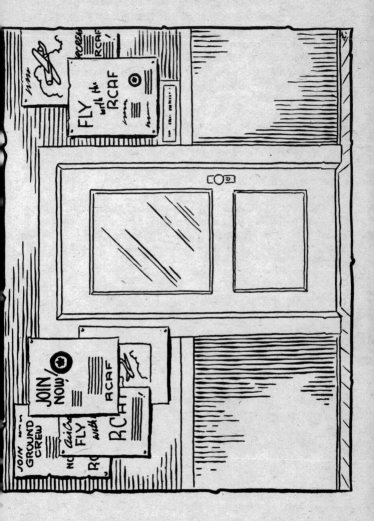

either friend or foe on the ground. In an attempt to secure safe passage for pilots flying over friendly lines, the Union Jack in the form of a shield was painted on the underside of British aircraft. Even though authorities later advocated the use of a larger Union Jack, the plan was eventually dropped altogether. At a distance, the St. George's cross in the Union Jack was difficult to distinguish from the German Cross.

The Royal Flying Corps, (RFC), then turned to their French allies for inspiration. The French had adopted a roundel based on the tricolour. The RFC and the Royal Naval Air Service took this roundel and reversed the colours, making the outer ring blue and the centre red. This same roundel has been carried on British aircraft ever since.

On November 30, 1921, the Canadian Air Force was presented with the Blue Ensign of the RAF to fly as their own. Lord Trenchard personally arranged the privilege, one that was retained by the RCAF at its formation on April 1, 1924. Other Commonwealth countries also adopted this ensign.

On July 5, 1940, the RCAF was authorized to introduce the maple leaf into the roundel in place of the round red centre. The roundel on the ensign was also revised: and it is now a blue ring surrounding a white area, in the centre of which is the red maple leaf.

*   *   *

The RAF and the RCAF owe their peculiar shade of air force blue to a curious source: the colour is that of the old Tsarist Russian uniform! England has always been a great supplier of continental uniforms (Napoleon's *Grande Armée* went to Moscow in greatcoats of English manufacture, so partial was the working of the continental blockade). At the time of the October Revolution in Russia there was a great quantity of cloth in England which had originally been ordered for the old Russian Army. It remained unused until it was utilized for the new service, which came into existence at the end of the First World War.

Cough and Go Aircrew

I can remember the excitement when I was a kid growing up in the western suburbs of Toronto, and the R-100 dirigible sailed majestically over our house. It was only travelling about fifty miles an hour – but what a thrill! It seemed to hover just above the roof tops, so low that we could see the crew waving back to us. From that day on I wanted to fly. Our childhood games of "I spy an airplane!" – the shout given by the first kid to spot one – became more serious. We began trying to identify those infrequently seen biplanes.

Today the subject is hardly worth a kid's attention. What with space shuttles, moon landings, and astronauts, it appears the kids of today have different reasons for wanting to fly. Here's what a grade five student out in Beausejour, Manitoba, wrote as a school essay:

When I grow up I want to be a pilot because it's a fun job and easy to do. That's why there are so many pilots flying around these days. Pilots don't need much school. They just have to learn to read numbers so they can read their instruments. I guess they should be able to read a road map, too.

Pilots should be brave so they won't get scared if it's foggy and they can't see, or if a wing or motor falls off. Pilots have to have good eyes to see through clouds and they can't be afraid of thunder or lightning because they are much closer to them than we are.

The salary pilots make is another thing I like. They make more money than they know what to do with. This is because most people think that flying a plane is dangerous, except pilots don't because they know how easy it is.

I hope I don't get air sick because I get car sick and if I get air sick I couldn't be a pilot and then I would have to work.

*   *   *

I went to private schools in British Columbia, and during my education I was warned not to use any "four letter words" and not to smoke, or I would get beaten by a prefect.

After joining the air force, straight from one of these schools, my first night in the RCAF was one of great shock. We were at the Manning Depot in Edmonton and I've never heard such swearing and rough language in my life. I can remember the first night, when I said my prayers by my bedside as I had been taught to do – even though I slept on the top bunk of a three tiered affair. *Dear God*, I said. *What am I doing here?*

Somehow, along with thousands of others, I survived the whole thing: the innoculations, the guard duty in the bitter cold, the line-ups for meals and pay … *and* the coarse, loud-mouthed Sergeant Major!

*   *   *

In the summer of 1940, recruiting for the air force was in full swing. Everyone wanted to fly after reading the daily exploits of pilots in the Battle of Britain. The thought that we wouldn't automatically be pilots never entered our heads.

It didn't take long for the air force to strip us of our delusions. Age, poor vision, colour blindness, flat feet, bunions, too much height, too little height – these and a host of other considerations decided the initial wartime fate of would-be pilots. A full and serious medical exam, called the "aircrew medical," did some more separating. Poor co-ordination, heart murmurs, a failure to blow long enough to pass the mercury test, hearing problems, suspect urine samples – the list seemed endless. A lot of would-be pilots were suddenly classified groundcrew.

For me it was "wireless." I was tremendously disappointed at the time, but with my eyesight I wonder now how I ever thought I could become aircrew. Off we went to Toronto to Manning Depot at the Exhibition Grounds. This was the infamous Bull Pen which housed many thousands of new recruits – all away from home for the first time and all as green as grass.

The Bull Pen had great light wells from the roof to the ground floor, since the floors were tiered. On the upper floors a balustrade had been erected to keep the guys from falling down the light shaft. This was made of two-by-fours and chicken wire, and was about eight feet high although it was open at the top. The washrooms hadn't been supplied with sinks, so tables with taps and tin basins were used. The basins were all bent and dented beyond belief and I wondered why. I found out the very first night.

Lights were turned out sharp at ten o'clock and everything went quiet. Most of the guys, tired out from a full day on the parade square, went instantly to sleep. We all came bolt upright when a sound like thunder broke the silence. Wash basins were being hurled over the chicken wire fence to crash far below on the concrete floor with a smashing and banging and ricochetting.

The security guards came running and yelling. They and the fire pickets began searching around, trying to find the culprits, while the rest of us silently enjoyed the show, lying in our bunks in the dark.

Finally, all went quiet again as everyone settled down and eventually went to sleep. That was when some daring soul who had smuggled a basin into his bunk, lobbed it into the light well where it fell with a hell of a crash. It started the guards chasing and cursing once more.

I never found out who those brave souls were who so early in our careers defied authority and put on the nightly entertainment. But I have always wished I knew.

*　*　*

One sometimes wonders, looking back, how you ever put up with all the characters you were thrust among in your training days. Our barracks contained just about every type of sleeper and sleep-walker: the guy who gnashed and ground his teeth all night; the arm waver; the leg pumper; the groaner; the many types of snorers; and the guy who yelled or screamed out in his sleep and scared the hell out of you.

All this happened after they supposedly had gone to sleep. Getting some of them into bed was another matter entirely. There was always one drunk who invariably staggered in shortly after the lights were turned out. Stumbling and crashing against the beds, he pawed his way around the room. There was an uproar as everyone woke up and told him just where to go.

We had one guy who had only just joined up. I think he was trying to prove he was a man by getting hammered every night. He'd come staggering in from the airmen's canteen, fall into bed with his clothes on, and then, a moment later, jump up and barf all over the floor. This would awaken everybody and they'd all start yelling for him to clean it up. After the same thing happened several nights in a row, I called a meeting.

We all laid down the law to this guy. Some even threatened violence. We thought our honker got the message for he promised to never do it again. But that very night – who did we see lurching his way towards the barracks? The barfer. He was earlier than usual so a few of us devised a plan. As soon as he hit the sack we would lift his bed and move it outside the hut, placing it on the grass beside the window where he normally slept. We followed through with our plan, and then we all returned inside and went to bed.

We had just gotten comfortably settled when we heard the window being pushed up. Then there was a rattle, a crash, a whoop, and a splash.

The poor guy, thinking he was inside and mindful of the penalty if he threw up on the floor, had heaved up the window and barfed in the same place as usual.

*   *   *

Our "H" hut had the usual washrooms. They were located upstairs and down in the bar of the H, so they were easily accessible to all. A long row of sinks was topped by a very narrow shelf where you could lay your razor, toothbrush, and so on. Above the shelf was an equally long and very thin continuous mirror that stretched the length of the room.

In the early morning traffic jam every basin was occupied, and there was a line of frantic guys jostling for position. Time was of the essence, for parades, like tides, wait for no man. At least not a lowly erk.

This particular morning, when we were lined up on the parade square ready for inspection, a French-Canadian guy called DesLaurier slid silently into position. But the Station Warrant Officer saw him out of the corner of his eye. During the inspection he stopped in front of DesLaurier and barked: "Did you shave this morning?"

DesLaurier put his hand to his chin and rubbed it.

"Put your hand down on parade!" roared the Warrant Officer. "Did you shave this morning?" he repeated.

DesLaurier replied: "I taught I 'ad, sir, but der were so many face in d'mirror, dat I might 'ave shave somebody else."

*   *   *

When I first arrived at Camp Borden in the 1920s it was loaded with characters. We had a Sergeant who was supposedly Jewish by persuasion. For a considerable time he enjoyed not only his own particular religious holidays but all others as well. Then somewhere along the line it was observed that he rarely, if ever, practised his religion, and the axe fell.

This Sergeant had two prized possessions. A brindle bulldog named Roscoe, and a 1928 five passenger Buick with two doors and "four-wheel" brakes. He lived in married quarters on the army side of the camp in what was then popularly known as "Syph" Row. The name came from the fact that the building had been a hospital for such cases during the First World War.

Invariably the Sergeant took Roscoe to work with him and just let the dog hang around until he had finished. Then, as a normal routine, they both headed for the wet canteen for a beer or two. Roscoe had a great thirst for beer and he lapped up his from a thundermug kept behind the bar for that purpose. After a beer or two he would always attempt to make love to the canteen cat – with great gusto but little success.

Roscoe had perhaps the shortest tail imaginable. It just managed to cover his "gonga chute." Although he loved to drink beer, it did strange things to his intestinal tract, and when you saw his tail rising very slowly, just like a thumb raised from a clenched fist, you knew it was time to keep your distance. He would let go with a hissing sound that was guaranteed to clear the bar area.

After their beer drinking session our hero and Roscoe would climb on board the Buick, with Roscoe taking his normal position on the rear window ledge. Away they would go down the gravel road to the main entrance but always, 100 yards or so down the road, the Buick would screech to a mighty stop. In a cloud of dust the car would careen out of its four-wheel skid, its door banging open. Out would fly Roscoe, a boot reaching for his rear in mid-air – and you knew that he had done it again.

*   *   *

Having survived our "nocs" and our first full week in the RCAF – all of it in quarantine – the next step for our eighty man intake was the Aircrew Selection Board.

High in the upper reaches of the hockey arena in Manning Depot at Edmonton sat a row of small offices, each occupied by a lone officer, rumoured to be a psychiatrist, in whose solitary hands rested our military destiny. We sat in the gloom of the unlit arena awaiting our alphabetical turn to be interviewed. None of us for a minute believed that we were going to be picked for anything but pilots. After all, we had passed our medicals that declared us physically fit standard aircrew, and we were keen as mustard. So what's to worry? But this was the fall of 1943 and bomber aircrew losses overseas were staggering. The need for replacements was becoming more crucial every day ... and there were two gunners in each bomber.

As each of our companions emerged from his brief encounter with the psychiatrist he was met with a chorus of, "What did you get?" It soon became clear that it was air gunner day, with possibly some wireless air gunners to sweeten the pot, and that there would be few, if any, chosen for pilot training.

I sank deeper into the gloom. There must be a way to avoid the fate of

my fellow-erks, I thought. And then it struck me. Don't ask to be a pilot – volunteer to become a navigator! Once you're selected as a navigator you can remuster later. Ah, the naivety of youth.

After a few more fellows passed through, each reappearing almost immediately with downcast eyes, it was my turn. I entered a small room to find a sombre looking Flying Officer wearing horn-rimmed glasses. He didn't bother to look up as I stepped to his desk and saluted smartly.

"I suppose you want to be a pilot, too," he said, not even trying to hide the exasperation in his voice.

"No, sir."

The officer paid no attention and pressed on. "And what makes you think you could make it as a pilot?"

"Sir, I'd like to be a navigator – "

"You kids are all the same, you all want to become fucking silk-scarf heroes – "

"But sir!" I broke in. "I want to be a navigator."

When my message sank in, the look of disbelief on his face was total. "What? You mean you don't want to be a pilot?"

"No, sir."

"Well, uh, ah, well," he sputtered, trying to recover his wits. "What do you know about aircraft?"

Here I turned on all burners, lying through my teeth. "Well, sir, I've been dreaming about flying since I was a kid. I've built all kinds of models, and I used to hang around airports just to watch the landings and takeoffs every chance I got." (Lies, all lies. I didn't know a Spitfire from a battleship.)

Just then the telephone rang in the next room.

"I'll be right back," the officer said.

While waiting for his return, I idly examined a small model aircraft sitting on the desk in front of me, noting the words "Hawker Hurricane" embossed on its underside. I had just replaced the model when the officer returned, obviously preoccupied with his thoughts.

"Yes, yes, where were we? Oh, yes, you're the one who wants to be a navigator, right? Tell me," he asked with a crafty look, "what's this aircraft?"

Like a shot, I replied: "The Hurricane, sir."

"Fine. Navigator it is. Send in the next man."

* * *

28

My selection as a navigator, instead of as a pilot, was a coincidence. Twenty-five of us transferred from the Forestry Corps to the RCAF. This was in England, and we all applied to be pilots.

At the Aircrew Receiving Centre in London we were examined for some days in the auditorium, which was a very narrow room about thirty-five feet long. We always filed in each day in the same order for the tests that would determine whether we should be gunners or pilots or bomb aimers or whatever.

The coincidence was that when we filed into the auditorium on that final day to hear our fate as aircrew, the first six in line became navigators and those behind became pilots. I never regretted being a navigator. But I was not impressed with the manner of deciding.

* * *

An awful lot of bomb aimers were really frustrated pilots. A lot of them had washed out of pilot training and now had to sit in the nose of a bomber and drop the bombs, when they knew in their heart of hearts that they could fly better than the guy at the controls. I made some notes on one conversation I had with my pilot.

"You're not very keen on flying, are you?" he asked.

"I'm positively not. I hate flying," I told him.

"Well, you shouldn't fly when your heart's not in it."

"That's my big problem. *Everyone* hates flying except the pilots."

"That's not true," the pilot answered. "I hope you haven't been speaking this way to my crew."

"They don't like it, either. None of the crews that I have flown with like it," I said.

"You're quite wrong there."

I was partly right. The navigator chimed in to say, "No one likes this game, but you just have to put up with it."

I agreed with him. Later that day, we did a bombing exercise. Though I tried my very best, the bombs fell all over the place. Afterwards, I heard the pilot say to the bombing leader: "He's not very keen on flying."

* * *

We were at Torquay in December 1945, waiting for a ship to take us home to Canada. It was just a holding unit. We only had to parade each morning for roll call and for the announcement of who was leaving on the next ship. People were arriving and departing every day so you never got to know anyone.

One morning I heard the Sergeant drone out: "Malcolm, Norris, Overend, Penfold, Quinn, Robinson, Skilton, Stott ... " Couldn't be Warren Skilton, could it? I thought. But it was an unusual name. Maybe his brother.

When the parade broke off I drifted down the parade square and was astounded to find my old school mate Jack Skilton.

"Skilton, you old bastard!" I yelled. "What in God's name are *you* doing in the RCAF?"

"Hello, George! It's great to see you. How have you been?"

"Skilton, how did you ever get in the RCAF?"

"What are you talking about? I got in like everyone else."

"Come on, Skilton, don't kid me. We went to school together for years ... even to Sunday school. I know you like my own brother. You're colour blind. You couldn't pass the medical exam!"

"Don't yell so loud, for God's sake. Yeah, well, maybe I am."

"So how did you ever pass the medical exam?"

"I had a sergeant friend who got a hold of that Japanese book the doctors all used – you know, the one with coloured dots all over a page – the dots formed a number? Yeah, well I memorized the numbers. I've been in the air force five years and nobody knows. Except you."

"You old bastard," I said, in admiration.

"Come on!" Skilton cried. "I'll buy the beer. What the hell does it matter now. The war's over!"

31

Circuits and Bumps

The first day a flight student and his instructor met was often a big one for both of them, and a time that was likely to be remembered.

I took a brand new cadet student into the hangar to show him the Chipmunk aircraft and to do a walk-around check. This kid was absolutely, frantically beside himself with keenness and enthusiasm. He could barely keep himself quiet.

Rounding the wing, I told him: "This – is the wing tip."

The student could contain himself no longer. "Yes, sir," he said, "but what does it do?"

"Well," I replied, "the goddamn thing has to end somewhere, doesn't it?"

*　　*　　*

The Elementary Flying Training School at High River, Alberta, had a rail line that passed one end of the field. It was just off the end of a runway, and most days when we flew over it the old, coal burning trains would be chugging along, belching smoke.

This particular day my student in the back seat was undershooting as we came in for a landing. I yelled into the gosport: "A little engine, a little engine!"

The student replied, "Yes, sir, I see it. I think it's the Chinook."

*　　*　　*

I told my pupil to climb up to 4,000 feet and level off. After a while, I noticed that he had climbed to 6,000 feet and showed no sign of levelling off. Curious, I called to him in the front cockpit. "How high are you, anyway?" I asked.

"Five feet, eight inches, sir," he replied.

*　　*　　*

One of the nice tricks some flying instructors had was to blow into the gosport tube that served as an intercom. This could wake you up in a hurry. They always did this before taking off in the old Tiger Moth, and you were ready for it – but they could catch you by surprise in the air.

Of course, the worst trick was for them to put the speaking tube out into the slipstream. This really hurt your ears!

*　　*　　*

The twenty hour check ride was always fear day for student pilots. Some of the students really got rattled just because it was a check. I took a poor guy up in a Cornell for his check one day.

On takeoff, the student see-sawed the rudder, finally giving it a left jab and yanking back on the control column. The strong left jab put us over the taxi strip and over other aircraft taxiing down wind. We had lurched into the air so I wasn't too worried – except he suddenly shoved the control column forward. (He had been taught to put the stick forward immediately on takeoff in order to gain airspeed.) This caught me unawares, and I found that our wheels were straddling one plane that was taxiing back for takeoff.

I didn't want the student to get upset at this stage of the flight, so I waited until we were about 500 feet in the air before asking: "Don't you think you were a little close to that plane when you took off?"

"Plane? What plane? I didn't see any plane."

I met the instructor of the other plane later in the mess, and he was still shaking.

*　　*　　*

Those training stations in wartime England! I thought that every new station I was posted to was worse than the last one. We were bullshitted into thinking that when you got on ops – oh, boy, *then* you'd have it made. But our operational stations were terrible, too. You had to walk so damn far to the mess hall or to operations. Most of the time it seemed you walked in the rain or the mud or both. If you weren't lucky enough to buy, beg, or steal a bicycle you really felt sorry for yourself.

And weren't those Nissen huts really something? The only heat you could get from the coke stoves was in trying to light the bloody things. It was just bloody marvellous to come back off a hairy op to those freezing huts and go to bed in your flying suit.... And those fucking straw pillows and straw filled pieces of mattress. I think they called them biscuits. You couldn't keep them on the springs, whatever they were called. I got so mad at the pillows I went out and bought a regular one at each station!

*　　*　　*

We were sent to Upper Heyford, near Oxford, for our Operational Training. Different crew members flew in Wellingtons at various exercises until our pilot had soloed; then we flew together as a crew. On the

36

days off I used to take the train to Oxford in the afternoon, returning at night. One time I took my bicycle along with me for some reason, and I was late getting back to the train station at Oxford. It was the last train that evening, so I bicycled right onto the platform as the train started to pull out. I jumped off and threw the cycle into the open door of a goods car – but unfortunately, as I tried to scramble into the train, the platform ran out. I missed the train and it was about a twelve mile walk back to base.

I never did get my bicycle back.

*   *   *

We had a meteorology instructor in England who was the classic case of "the war must go on." Nothing less than a maximum effort would ever do – total victory and victory at any cost, sort of thing.

His method of delivering a lecture was similar to and hardly more effective than a tape recording, but it occupied every second of the time allotted. He started to speak the moment he entered the classroom, and was saying his last word as the door closed behind him.

One day a German fighter made a sweep over Eastbourne, letting fly with cannon and machine guns. As he neared our building our instructor, at the last split second, interrupted his lecture and joined us all in diving under the desks.

Of course, by the time we had taken cover the German had gone. Before we had a chance to get out from under the desks our meteorologist was continuing his spiel as if nothing had happened.

His only reference to the episode was to mention the fact that he had gone beyond his allotted time by forty-five seconds. For which he apologized.

*   *   *

We were training to be air gunners and flew first in Fairey Battles. Later they were retired, and we switched to Blenheims. Three air gunners flew together and each in turn fired off two belts, one for each Browning machine gun. When one gunner finished firing at the drogue, another gunner would feed his belts into the guns and take his turn in the turret.

Loading each belt separately like that took too much time, so two of us decided to join our belts together. This would speed things up and get

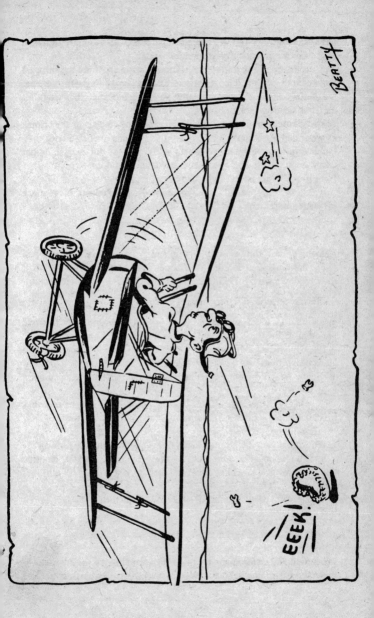

us back on the deck sooner. We joined the belts with an empty cartridge case from a previously fired round.

After my buddy had fired his 300 rounds I moved into the turret. I attempted to load the guns, but try as I might I couldn't get the cocking handle back. When I told the pilot we had a blockage that wouldn't clear, he headed back to base.

The station armourers had been alerted and they met us on the tarmac as we rolled up. After we explained that the guns wouldn't cock they climbed into the turret to see for themselves. They did everything but take the guns and turret apart – and they still couldn't understand how a fired round could be left in a chamber of a gun.

Needless to say we didn't enlighten them, but wandered off to more pleasant amusement.

* * *

Remember the "rumble fund"? I think every flying training station had one. Each time a student pulled a boner – taxied with his flaps down, took off down wind, or committed some other gaffe – he had to ante up. Usually the fine was fifty cents but some fines went as high as five dollars.

One New Zealander became famous on our station. He got fined every time he touched an aircraft. Every time the poor guy flew we would all gather outside to see how many fines he would get.

One day we had all gathered to watch him do a landing, and we were all wondering out loud how much the old party fund was going to benefit. We had a pair of binoculars and the guy using them started a running commentary.

"He has his wheels down. He has his flaps down. God, he even has his canopy open … that saves him fifty cents. Will he remember to raise his flaps before taxiing?"

We all watched the aircraft touch down and turn off the runway.

Soon our announcer, who could see the action in the cockpit, reported that the pilot was reaching down for the flap lever. Then he said in a small voice: "Oh, oh."

We all watched as the aircraft sank slowly into the runway. The pilot had pulled up his wheels.

* * *

I was positive I was going to get my Wings, for I had passed my Elementary Flying Training School with good marks. Now I was off to Service

Flying Training School at Brandon, Manitoba, and twin Cessna aircraft.

But it seemed to me that it was just as nerve wracking trying to solo on the twins as on the single engined Moths. However, I did it one day; and my confidence grew with each additional flight. I remember that I once had a "hairy" after coming back from a cross country solo. A strong wind had come up, as well as a bit of a cross wind. Perhaps you will remember that to speed things up at training fields we used to land on one runway and take off on another. The two runways in this case were parallel to each other, some thirty feet apart. I came in with extra throttle and with a slight allowance for the cross wind, but unfortunately I hit the runway rather hard and bounced back up into the air. The aircraft started to slide towards the takeoff runway. In a state of bewilderment and shock I gunned both engines to go round again. Sweat was pouring from me as I came in for my second attempt. When the aircraft touched down I breathed a sigh of relief.

I wondered if the guys in the control tower would give me hell for my poor flying, but they never did. I went into the hangar and the flight room, got a Coke, and sat as quiet as I could to relax. I had hardly taken a seat when another student pilot burst into the room. "Jesus!" he cried. "Did you see that? I was about to take off and some idiot landed right in front of me!"

"No kidding," I said softly. And looked the other way.

*   *   *

It was our Wings graduation party. The endless training and straining to be a pilot was finally over. All the sweat and tears were behind us. Those Wings over our left breast pockets were proof to all the world of our new status, especially noticeable, we hoped, to the feminine gender. Around each sleeve of our new officer uniforms was the single thin braid that proclaimed we were Pilot Officers. We were all nineteen feet tall – and we were also still suffering from the all-hours stag party of the night before.

One of our group had arranged for his girlfriend in town to get dates for all of us. All we had to do was pick up the four girls and bring them out to the base where the graduation dance was being held. Resplendent in our new uniforms, our newly won Wings seeming to glow from our chests, we arrived at the girlfriend's house. As we got out of the car I felt a horrible pressure begin cramping my bowels. *Oh, no*, I thought.

We were all crowded together on the verandah saying our hellos to the four girls and a set of parents when I felt the dreaded rush of warmth envelope me. As quickly and calmly as I could, without waiting for introductions, I asked to use the bathroom and was shown to the top of the stairs.

Once the bathroom door closed I began to breathe again. As swiftly as possible I proceeded to remove my laden underwear and to perform such ablutions as I could, under the circumstances. I guess I was taking too much time for I heard a light tapping on the door. Then a female voice asked if everything was all right. My heart stopped but I was able to reassure her that everything was just fine and that I would be right down. I began to work in a panic. What the hell was I going to do with this underwear? I wondered.

Flushing it down the toilet would only bung up the plumbing. Ah, the window! One quick toss and it would disappear forever. It was a great plan – except that I couldn't get the window up. As I strained to raise it I noticed that it had frosted glass panes and many layers of paint.

A chorus of voices yelled at me from below to hurry up. Now I really panicked. Giving one desperate heave I broke the paint seal and forced the window up just enough to get my arm out. Then with one deft twist of my wrist I sent the hated, soggy mess flying through the air.

What a fantastic relief. I hammered the window down with my fist, carefully washed my hands, and combed my hair. I straightened my tunic and centred my belt buckle. Then, as nonchalantly as possible, I descended the stairs and went merrily outside to where everyone was waiting at the car.

I stepped off the verandah to find a rather stunned group standing around in a semi-circle. There, at their feet, was my horrible looking pair of shorts.

Celestial Bodies

Guys on our squadron in England were always trading things when they weren't borrowing things ... like money or bicycles or motorcycles or wrecks of cars.

Perhaps the best trade of the war, that I ever heard of, was the swap of a girlfriend for a motorbike. A pilot had a real smashing girlfriend, a real doll, and everyone was envious. A rear gunner offered him a motorbike in trade for her. As part of the bargain the pilot had to promise that he would not accept any more invitations to her home for dinner, and that he wouldn't call her up or go out with her again.

I'm not sure, but I think he sold the bike for fifty pounds when he left the squadron.

*   *   *

We had a guy in the Air Division who was so smart-looking he made Steve Canyon, of comic book fame, look homely. He, too, was a blond with a well-developed body, and he had his uniforms hand-tailored to emphasize his masculinity. He always looked like he was going on parade. Dashing. The French girls openly stared at him on the streets and to top it all off he was fluent in the French language. Some catch.

The great thing was that he was unaffected by the stir and fluttering he caused in those female hearts. He was just one of the boys, and spent most of his time in the airmen's canteen with his pals.

One day our hero, while in town shopping, met a beautiful French girl. They soon became quite fond of each other. The girl was the only daughter of a French Count, whose fortune had been rather savagely battered by the war. Nevertheless the Count and Countess still lived on the family's large, if rundown, estate. As the expression goes they were "in straitened circumstances."

As everyone who has lived in France knows, to be invited to a French home for dinner is a great and signal honour and so to be treated. In all good time our hero got his invitation to dinner. He knew exactly what this signified; everything would have to be premier class.

Late in the appointed afternoon our hero drove his tiny convertible through the wrought-iron gates of the estate and up the long, circular, tree lined drive towards the mansion. As he approached closer he could see the beautiful daughter, plus the Count and Countess, standing in front of the long steps leading to the entrance.

It was then our hero decided to vent some rumbling stomach gases brought on by a long night in the Wets. But time was of the essence, he

47

must do it quickly, before his car reached the steps. As fate would have it the pressure was too great. The manoeuvre failed.

Now he was upon the assembled nobility. He could see that they had drinks in hand, that they were smiling at him. The beautiful daughter leaned forward eagerly.

Our hero smiled weakly back at them, gave a tiny wave of his hand and, with gravel spurting, gunned away down the drive.

He never went back.

* * *

On a snowy winter's night in London during the war, two Canadian pilots wanted to take a WAAF (a member of the Women's Auxiliary Air Force), up to their hotel room. Those were the days when eagle-eyed hotel clerks patrolled the premises, checking on untoward happenings in their sacred rooms. It took ingenuity of a high order to smuggle a girl past the hotel desk.

Our heroes decided that one of them would undress in the alley beside the hotel, so the girl could wear his uniform over her own. Then, when the girl and one pilot got safely to the room, they would throw the uniform out the window to the guy in the alley. The plan worked perfectly as one pilot and the girl, dressed in the officer's uniform with greatcoat, sauntered casually through the lobby and up the elevator.

Meanwhile, the unlucky pilot was freezing to death in the alley. Finally their window went up, and a head appeared. Then a shower of uniform landed on him. All of the uniform, that is, except the pants. They had landed halfway down, caught on a wire. Still, with the greatcoat covering most of his bare legs, the pilot managed to enter the hotel and reach their room.

In the morning, a five pound note slipped to a friendly porter got the pants off the wire, and our heroes departed the hotel triumphant.

* * *

The pilot prepared to start the engines. As he reached for the switches, a small bird flew in the open window of the aircraft and perched on his shoulder. The pilot's surprise grew as the bird spoke to him and said: "I wouldn't start the engines if I were you, sir. The undercarriage mechanism is U/S."

In shocked surprise the pilot checked immediately with the groundcrew

48

and soon discovered that a serious fault in the undercarriage mechanism would undoubtedly have caused a bad crash on landing. As he turned to leave, the pilot again noticed the little bird and thanked his feathered friend for the astounding advice.

"Think nothing of it," said the little bird. "I couldn't let you take off knowing the aircraft was unserviceable. You see, actually I'm an airwoman, but a wicked witch cast a spell over me and I must remain like this until the spell is broken."

"But how can the spell be broken?" asked the pilot.

"Well, sir, if you could take me to your quarters and in the witching hour place me carefully on your pillow ... I shall be free of the curse and will resume my former shape when the clock strikes."

The pilot was much moved by this and, feeling that he owed a deep debt of gratitude, he carefully lifted the little bird and took it to his quarters. There he waited, and at the appointed witching hour placed the little bird tenderly on his pillow....

It is unfortunate that the court martial would not believe a word of the story.

*   *   *

At Hibaldstow, where I was working as a WAAF flight mechanic in 1945, it was a flight order that, in rough weather, one of the ground staff was to sit on the tail of each Spitfire as it taxied from the dispersal to the distant runway in order to prevent the wind from tipping the aircraft over on its nose.

On this occasion, my pilot did not receive the order "Rough Weather Procedure," which was issued from Flying Control. Not having seen me jump up on the tailplane while the other mechanics removed the chocks, he did not wait for me to descend when he reached the runway. Instead, he took straight off.

The violently increased rate at which we were taxiing first told me that something was wrong, and I flung myself across the fuselage and grasped the elevator in an attempt to attract the pilot's attention. I was unable to move it. Events move quickly with a Spitfire. There seemed only a panic-stricken moment before the end of the rushing sensation of travelling along the runway told me that we were actually airborne.

At that moment I was not merely in great danger. I was, to all practical purposes, already dead. I had no hold other than that of three fingers, which I had managed to get around the cutaway portion of the tailplane;

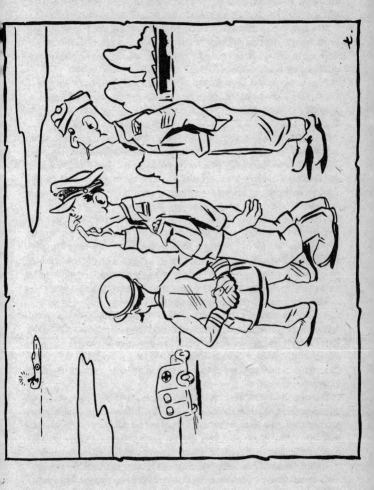

there was no possibility of attracting the attention of either the pilot or anyone on the ground; and it seemed so certain that I must roll off the fuselage the first time the aircraft banked, that I did not even trouble to wriggle farther across it to balance the weight of my heavy boots.

It was at this moment of realization that fear left me. Newbolt knew what he was writing about when he described the traveller who was doomed to certain death by the brigands into whose hands he had fallen, as spending his last hours "in a dream untroubled of hope."

My first coherent thought was, *I've muffed it for the last time. Better me than most people, but I wish it hadn't happened!* There was nothing much stronger than that: a passing regret – you may laugh if you like, but it's true – that my NAAFI* cigarette and chocolate rations would be wasted; and a deeper regret that I could not leave a message to tell my mother how easy death had been. Strangely, although I realized that my family would feel my loss, there was no conviction that I was leaving them. Of anxiety for what was to come there was none, though I have never been any braver than the next person, and I am a funk when it comes to climbing ladders or riding bicycles.

The force of the slipstream must have been terrific, for there was nothing but that and the precarious hold of my fingertips to prevent me rolling forward, though the fin made it impossible to slip over the tail of my mount. Before many minutes there was a sensation of blood rushing to my head, a feeling of something pressing me down, and a blackness before my eyes. I thought with a mild sense of gratitude that death was coming in the easy form of a "black-out" ....

There was never any sensation of the mist dissolving. My next recollection is of a perfectly clear head and an entirely fresh line of thought. The doctrine that good is the source of all power, while evil is a figment of our imagination, was something that had long appealed to my reason. Now (my own voice seemed to be saying in my ear), was the chance to prove it.

Steadily the idea that there was nothing to harm me took possession of my mind, helped by the clear serene sky. I knew I was safe whether the flight was to last ten minutes or a couple of hours. Shortly afterwards, I felt the aircraft drop – so gently that I did not realize the cause until the returning sensation of speed proclaimed that we were back on the runway.

As we slowed down I slipped off the tailplane, ran back for my beret (which had remained faithfully on my head until we reached the ground),

*Navy Army Air Force Institute

52

and made my way back across the grass to the dispersal. The pilot taxied home round the perimeter road, still unaware why his controls had refused to function.

How, in the circumstances, he achieved that perfect landing I have never understood, but he must have had a harrowing ten minutes in the air. On leaving the runway he had found his elevator almost unserviceable, and after struggling round the circuit at 600 feet had radioed for permission to land.

The Flying Control officer, who had, only that moment, been informed by the Flight Office of my predicament, judged it safest not to tell the pilot of the presence of a passenger. It was not until he walked indignantly into the Flight Office to report his aircraft U/S that he learned that he had been the victim of an unusual case of "parasite drag."

Whatever his feelings, he was off with the next detail, and I should have accompanied him – to the beginning of the runway only – if he had not implored me, as I prepared to scramble up: "I know you don't want to lose your nerve ... but please don't come on my tail again!"

* * *

I was a fabric worker. I remember a prank that one of the boys played on us girls, while we were rib stitching fabric to a Canso aileron.

The aileron was sitting on a trestle; and while several of us were working on the outside, one of our girls was actually inside the aileron. A groundcrew chap decided to put an air hose up inside her overall pant leg.

Well, if you've never seen an aileron fly all by itself you really have missed something! That aileron took off with the girl inside and flew right out of the hangar, knocking everyone and everything out of its way.

When it landed outside the hangar neither it nor its unwilling passenger was harmed. But the girl was livid. She got out and dusted herself off and came into the hangar by a rear door. Did she ever chase after that prankster!

* * *

One of the disasters of wartime WAAF uniforms was the button-fastened panties that were issued. Since elastic was rationed, the panties were secured by a single button which had a great habit of popping at the wrong time.

My girlfriend and I were strolling along to the barracks one day after lunch, when we both watched her button fall to the ground and roll ahead of us.

I gave her a safety pin and she ducked into the drill hall to attend to her needs. She stepped backwards into the doorway, upped her skirt, fastened the panties with the pin, and pulled her skirt down. But before she could step out of the doorway she heard thunderous clapping and cheering behind her. She turned to find 500 men on parade – all delighted at her sudden appearance before them.

*   *   *

Anyone who has travelled by car through France knows how difficult it is to find a washroom. Thus, while she was taking a trip by car, it was at a village inn that the RCAF airwoman stopped to inquire of mine host, in her uncertain French: "*Le* washroom, *s'il vous plaît, m'sieu?*"

He studied her Canadian uniform thoughtfully for a moment, clucked his tongue, then replied: "Ah, I regret, *mademoiselle* – today I have only the Pepsi-Cola!"

*   *   *

Lots of people have fallen into the Atlantic Ocean; some with airplanes, some from boats, and some on purpose – although not usually in December. I, however, am probably the only person who has almost fallen in with a whole load of air force garbage.

It happened in 1942, around Christmas time, when I was in the Women's Division of the RCAF and drove a car in Torbay, which is in Newfoundland. The Mechanized Transport section was short of drivers that day, so I was "joed" for the station garbage run. At first this seemed to me sort of "cushy" for, as usual, it was snowing like anything and the wind was shrieking around the buildings. It was, I felt, much better than taking the Duty Run to St. John's, six rocky miles away, and doing all sorts of futile errands for people who should have done them for themselves.

I went out to the garage where "Irma" slept (she was a Chevy dump-truck), tapped the gas gauge, and started her up. After a few abortive attempts I even got her dump mechanism to work. I did notice that I never knew whether I was in low or reverse but I didn't think much of it at the time. Then I picked up the official garbage collector at the Station

54

Warrant Officer's office. He, of course, was to do the actual collecting; after all, I had a trade and couldn't be expected to come into actual contact with the garbage. However, he was awfully small and quite a bit younger than me, so in the end we were both heaving all kinds of junk onto my dump, and I was rapidly peeling off mounds of clothing.

Fortunately, I could do a certain amount of strip-tease with great propriety. I was wearing a set of airmen's underwear, a pair of battledress pants (two sizes too big), a turtleneck sweater, a tartan scarf of the clan MacDhu (it said so on the label), an airmen's parka with hood, a pair of fifteen-dollar sheepskin gloves (a present from my mother, "in case your hands get cold"), and a pair of old-type flying boots. Incidentally, all winter long, whenever I met the Women's Division officer, I had to leap into the snowdrifts and salute smartly with my legs hidden. I have often wondered what she must have thought of me, but then all of us in Newfie were slightly demented. It was the thing.

In about an hour my friend and I had collected quantities of garbage, plus three cups of coffee, two chocolate bars, and several snorts of Drambuie. (I can't say where I got the last, of course, but it wasn't at the officers' mess; they were never as generous as the sergeants.) The time had come to dump!

Imagine my horror when Junior directed me to the cliffs at Torbay. Even my fifteen-dollar hands grew numb. I didn't feel I knew Irma well enough to ask her to lean over cliff edges, particularly backwards. I should explain, by the way, that Torbay Station was a mile or so inland, and that the village lay in a hollow between two cliffs beside the sea. A perfect dumping place for garbage – provided *I* wasn't driving Irma.

Nevertheless, in due course, we ground our way up to the top of the cliff, stopped on the road, and surveyed the tossing Atlantic as it crashed on the rocks far below. Only six inches of grass separated the road from that abyss. I backed Irma to the edge and, with much grinding and clashing, upended my garbage into the briny. Feeling rather pleased, I brought the dump back into position and glanced out at my rear wheels. One glance was enough. Shuddering, I prepared to advance to safety. And then a terrible thing happened. I couldn't remember which was low and which was reverse gear, and there was no room for error – none at all. I examined the gears at length and simply couldn't bring myself to do anything. We sat there for some time. Junior was very sympathetic but he couldn't help.

We'd probably still be there, encrusted with three feet of salt and serving as a National Historic Site had not an American soldier heaved into sight, complete with gun and bristling police dog. This nice man showed me the right gear and even turned my truck around for me while I guarded Newfoundland by holding his gun and his dog. I'm terribly glad he didn't go over the brink.

Junior and I returned to the station just in time for lunch, and to my intense relief I was told that Irma had to have her 1,000 mile check that afternoon. Heaven only knows what happened to the rest of the garbage.

I've got lots of interesting stories about driving around Torbay. There was the time when 120 parcels of clean officers' laundry (that is, officers' clean laundry), fell out of a panel truck *en route* to St. John's. There was a certain trip to Cape Spear with beer, which was very exciting .... We drivers were like the Mail: nothing stopped us – though I must admit that the officers' laundry was rather a blot on our record. But, since I myself got by with a turtleneck sweater, and only used a shirt on Sundays when I sang in the choir, I never quite understood why the Adjutant had to make such a fuss about it all!

Dinner at Seven

A Mess Dinner in the officers' mess was a most formal occasion. It called for full RCAF dress uniform and, in the old days, was a stag affair. Each one followed the same set pattern – a procedure set in stone, once each month. If you were part of a large station your turn to attend only came up a few times a year.

The formal attire that had to be worn was so theatrical it rendered the event a command performance and instilled a desire for prankish humour. It is doubtful if anyone could dream up a more uncomfortable rig.

Extremely narrow-legged and tight trousers, so highly cut they demanded suspenders rather than belts, were fitted over quarter Wellington boots. The legs were so tight that the elastic loop on the bottom of each pant leg could only be manoeuvred over the boots by a clever stratagem. First, you sat down and pulled your pants on, but only halfway. Then you put your boots on, and slipped the elastic bands over the boots. Then you stood up and pulled up the trousers. This drew the pants, with their gold braided stripes, as tight as your crotch could bear. They were so straight that it was difficult to bend your legs or to sit down.

A tiny tunic, separated from the trousers by a cummerbund, had rank stripes of gold braid on each sleeve. Of course, miniature medals were always worn. Under the tunic was a boiled white shirt, a stiff, detached, wing collar, and a black bowtie. The shirt was the kind that pulls over your head and has holes for four gold studs.

So attired, you gathered with your fellow officers in the anteroom of the mess for pre-dinner drinks. In a far corner of the mess a string quartet played martial airs. Smoking was not permitted until the King or Queen had been toasted, which always caused a traffic jam in the lavatory.

At seven o'clock, a piper in full Highland regalia piped the long line of officers, led by the senior officers and guests of honour, into the dining room. Everything was spit and polish. Everyone sternly correct and on his best behaviour. The room gleamed and glistened from the reflections of the candles on the silverware, crystal, cut glass, and resplendent uniforms. Following a brief word from the padre everyone was seated according to a pre-arranged seating plan.

When the King or Queen had been toasted, the port wine and cigars were circulated. This was the moment everyone had longed for for hours, and a great gasping and blowing filled the room as everyone lit up and dragged madly at cigarettes or cigars. As hard as the no smoking rule was it didn't come close to the rule which forbade anyone to leave the room during the dinner. It added an agonizing dimension to the long, drawn-out meal.

Usually, each Mess Dinner included a guest speaker who would drone on about something or other. They, for some reason, were never noted for their intellectual excellence, although why they weren't raises an interesting point. Following the speech, everyone filed out to the ante-room and proceeded to hammer back the drinks – but not before hammering the doors off the lavatory in their haste to enter.

Then it was party time. Cards, dice, pool, or the more robust drinking contests. While each Mess Dinner more or less followed this set routine, there were occasional unexpected and startling exceptions.

One dinner was proceeding nicely at RCAF Station Lachine when I felt the officer next to me on my left grab my hand below the table. He whispered, "Tie your napkin on!" I looked down to see the end of a long "rope" made from the large linen napkins we were using. I had no idea what was going on.

I began silently tying my napkin onto the end of the rope while getting sidelong glances from my fellows, urging me to hurry. I passed the end of the rope to the guy on my right and whispered the necessary directions. Meanwhile, we were all apparently sitting sedately and nonchalantly, proceeding with our meals. The tables had been set in a U shape with the bottom of the U forming the head table. Here the CO and his guests of honour were seated with other senior officers. I wondered what would happen when the rope reached the guy sitting next to the head table.

I didn't have long to wonder. A whisper passed swiftly up the row: "Tell him to tie the rope onto the tablecloth of the head table." The message was passed and we all sat waiting. This was the crucial moment. If the rope wasn't tied to the tablecloth all had been in vain. We continued to eat silently, one hand on the rope.

Finally down the line came the whispered message: "It's tied!"

Quickly everyone dropped both hands onto the rope and the word, "Pull!" floated up the row. I pulled with the rest of them but my eyes were firmly fixed on the CO, who was busy, at that moment, explaining something to a guest.

With one mighty heave the tablecloth came flying towards us and the head table seemed to leap upwards. Steaks, wine, candles, butter, vegetables, cutlery, and curses flew in all directions, as the bare wood of the table suddenly appeared.

The CO rose, half up and half down from his chair, his mouth open, his arm outstretched, finger pointing as though issuing a command. But not a word escaped him, and slowly and silently he sank back into his chair, his shirt front stained red with the wine and gravy and vegetables that had been splattered up his arms and across his tunic. The room was in an uproar, everyone talking at once. Our row was the exception. We sat very dignified and silent, leaning forward with curious stares on our questioning faces as we watched the leaping gyrations of the senior officers who were trying to escape the deluge.

The kitchen staff hustled out as though this was routine procedure. Soon everything was restored to subdued and dignified order, and the Mess Dinner proceeded.

One other memorable night a "floor show" was staged. Two junior officers did the acting. The purpose of the one-act play was to impress a very senior and pompous member of the federal government, who was the guest of honour that evening.

Midway through the dinner, one of the juniors began acting drunk. He started shouting and banging on the table. Those seated around him all tried to shush him up, but they no sooner got him quieted down when he would burst forth again.

The CO and his guest began to take an interest as our actor got fully into the swing of things. His remarks grew louder and more vulgar and more incoherent. Finally, the guest of honour became visibly disturbed. He could be seen motioning in the direction of the actor as he talked to the CO.

No longer able to tolerate the commotion, the CO barked at the President of the Mess Committee: "Mr. PMC, control that man!"

The PMC rose at his place at the end of the head table and yelled down its length to the other actor, who was the Vice PMC: "Mr. Vice, control that man!"

The VPMC stood up and said: "Yes, sir!" With that, he pulled a gun from his back pocket, pointed it at his raving partner, and fired.

The roar and flash of the .38 revolver shook the room and startled everyone. We all stared, bug-eyed in horror, as our actor staggered away from his chair, clutching his chest. Letting out a piercing scream, he fell backwards. They couldn't do it better in Hollywood.

Chalk white, the guest of honour leaped to his feet. "My God!" he cried. "He's killed the man!"

* * *

I knew I was drunk. The realization hit me the moment I stepped out of the officers' mess on Gloucester Street into the cold, dark night.

I also knew I had to be very careful, for the Ottawa police had dou-

bled their Christmas season patrols looking for drunk drivers. The Mayor had said there would be no warnings given, no leniency. Everyone would be jailed. The air force itself got into the act and dire warnings had been issued by the Air Member for Personnel. Drunk driving would not be tolerated. If found guilty, you were liable to be thrown out of the service.

The fact that the Air Member for Personnel had been picked up two nights after his announcement and slapped in jail, somehow reinforced the warning. After we all got over laughing about it.

I had parked my car directly across from the entrance to the mess, and I gingerly made my way to it through the curbside snowdrifts. I can remember cursing the narrow tight-legged pants of my mess dress uniform. They were so tight they almost prevented your legs from bending. But over everything else my brain was whispering: *You're drunk, stupid, so be careful. Get in your car and drive very slowly, otherwise you're a dead duck.*

I crept out onto Bank Street and began carefully and slowly turning south, trying my best to be alert to the traffic. As I turned my head a whistle shattered my ear drums, and a giant policeman jumped in front of my headlights, hand raised. "Stop!" he roared.

My heart went into my boots. Oh, Jesus, why me?

With one bound the cop yanked open the passenger door and landed beside me. "Follow that car!" he yelled, pointing ahead. "Hurry up, man, he's just robbed the drug store!"

I couldn't see any car ahead of us but I jammed down the accelerator and we tore up the street to begin the wildest ride of my life. I never did see any car ahead of us no matter how hard I looked, but I followed instructions.

"Turn here. Faster, faster, man, he's getting away! Watch out for that car. Come on, faster!" The policeman had his nose pressed on the windshield, his eyes staring ahead, and I don't believe he ever looked at me.

When the cop had decided we weren't going to catch anyone he told me to pull over so that he could get out. He stood there with the car door open and thanked me over and over again.

"It's citizens like you who make our job easier. Good night, sir."

"Good night, officer," I replied. And I drove home cold, cold sober.

*   *   *

I flew my ops on Hally Bags out of Eastmoor on 415 squadron. We had a stand down one day. It was just before payday and our crew only had a few bob between us, but we decided, what the hell, let's go to town anyway.

As we were finishing our beer at the first pub a fly landed on my glass. I caught it and tossed it into the dregs of the beer. Then I proceeded to the bar, and in a loud voice demanded to know of the pub owner what kind of beer he was serving – with flies in it!

The owner was profuse in his apologies and offered me another beer. I said I could only accept his apology and a "clean beer" if he also bought a round for my crew.

This worked so well that we all proceeded on a pub crawl. We made sure, of course, that we had a new fly for each pub. It was a great night.

*　　*　　*

I remember loading up on beer one night in town and then getting on the bus back to the station. Halfway home I thought my bladder was going to burst, so I ran up and told the bus driver to stop and let me out. He opened the door and I got out to relieve myself on the side of the road. Soon, half the bus passengers were standing alongside of me, all with the same idea. The WAAF's sort of looked the other way.

*　　*　　*

I was an air gunner flying Lysanders in France in 1939-40. All the air gunners were erks in those phoney war times, so you got "joed" for a lot of menial jobs. One of the more tedious tasks was guard duty during the night hours. Two men would pair off and, complete with full web equipment, full water bottles, and loaded rifles with fixed bayonets, would guard the aircraft.

On this particular night my friend and I had repaired to a local *estaminet* for a meal during our four hours off duty. After our meal, my friend emptied out his water bottle and filled it with Old Nick rum. Then we went back to guarding the aircraft.

About 0300 hours the Orderly Officer made his rounds, accompanied by the Orderly Sergeant. After being properly challenged, he asked me, "Is your water bottle full?"

"Yes, sir," I answered.

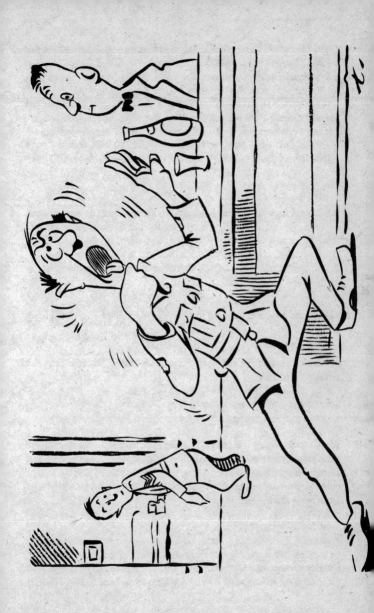

The Orderly Officer shook it to prove the point, and then said to my friend, "Is your bottle full?"

"Yes, sir," was the response.

"May I have a drink from your bottle? I'm very thirsty."

"Yes, sir," replied my friend, who, with some hesitation, removed his water bottle from his belt and handed it to the Orderly Officer.

The Orderly Officer took a long pull from the bottle. After recovering his breath a few minutes later, he gasped: "That's damned good water. It's a good job I didn't ask what the bottle was full of!"

*   *   *

It was real easy in those days to get twenty-one days CB – confined to barracks. Of course, during the war, the food in England was atrocious. Remember how the Orderly Officer accompanied by the Orderly Sergeant would visit the mess hall each meal and ask, "Any complaints?" Some guys were foolish enough to answer and always wound up doing extra duty or being CB'ed.

At one training station in England the Orderly Officer was a real "pukka" type, complete with handle-bar mustache. One day, we were served tripe, and when the Orderly Officer asked for complaints, my buddy stood up. Over marched the Orderly Officer and the Orderly Sergeant. "Yes? What is it?" the officer demanded.

Pointing at the tripe my friend asked, "Is this to be eaten or has it already been eaten?"

He got twenty-one days confined to barracks.

*   *   *

But there was some good food in England. You have never eaten ambrosia until you have savoured real fish and chips served in newspaper and eaten with your fingers on your long walk home to base. And who cared whether the fish was haddock, halibut, or hake – as long as the chips were made from Small Majestics.

*   *   *

One of the most annoying jobs a junior officer got stuck with was Orderly Officer duty. You couldn't drink while on duty (at least you weren't supposed to), and you couldn't leave the base for twenty-four

hours. To kill time you usually hung around the mess watching the other officers drinking or playing pool or cards.

When closing time came for the various bars and canteens you had to collect the night's receipts and lock them away. You also had to ensure that the Orderly Corporal and the Orderly Sergeant supervised the fire pickets and sundry other small chores. Combined with your day's normal work it made for a long and tiring stint.

On nights when the mess had a planned entertainment, a dance or bingo or some special "do," you would usually retire to the room reserved for the Orderly Officer, which contained a bed, a chair, and a telephone.

My turn for Orderly Officer duty came one night when the annual Christmas bingo was being held in the mess. The place was jammed with enthusiastic bingo fans, and guys you hadn't seen for months came out of the woodwork to try to win a turkey. I was cajoled into joining a table occupied by some friends, although I loathed the game. But it was better than sitting in the Orderly Officer's room.

It happened that two of my drinking buddies were handling the bingo and calling out the numbers. They made great sport of the fact that I was sitting there, soberly putting chips on numbers, while they were imbibing and playing Bob Hope with the microphone.

At half time the bingo stopped for the customary breather, and the two bingo callers put down the microphone to pay me a visit. They stood behind me and criticized my bingo card, wondering how I could be so stupid as to play with such a dumb specimen. They were having a grand time reading out my numbers and laughing and horsing around. Since I wasn't in the best of humour I told them to piss off.

When play resumed I put markers on the first four numbers called: fourteen … twenty-six … fifty-one … seventy-two. "Bingo!" I shouted. The room erupted. Some people yelled that it was not possible to have a bingo with only four numbers. Others just said *merde*. But it was true. Including the centre free space there were five numbers in a straight line.

I couldn't believe my luck.

A week later I was standing at the bar when my two bingo-calling friends rolled in. I hadn't seen them since the bingo game, and they wanted to know if the turkey I had won tasted okay.

"Just great! I don't think I've ever eaten a juicier bird. It really was great," I enthused. Then I noticed both of them grinning at me in a funny way. "What the hell are you two grinning about?" I demanded.

They said, in unison: "Fourteen, twenty-six, fifty-one, seventy-two."

I can still remember staring incredulously as the message slowly sank in, and my stomach gave a funny heave.

"You bastards," I said.

People Are Special

One thing remains with you after finishing a military career. People.

Events, places, and battles tend to blur with age. People, special people, remain fresh in your mind's eye, bright and clear and often beautiful. Those visions warm as you grow older. Some become as mellow as an autumn sun. Military service has no finer reward.

Colin was a dreamer, a gentle dreamer. He had been a pilot in the RAF during the war, and after emigration to Canada he joined the RCAF in 1948.

Like a lot of us who had re-entered the RCAF, he was newly married and strapped for cash. We were all trying to start married life on a shoelace, and we were living from payday to payday. Our new brides were not expected to work; wasn't done, you know.

Colin and I were posted to 408 Photographic Squadron at Rockcliffe, then gearing up for the massive job of mapping northern Canada. Our summers were spent flying the old Lancaster bombers all over the Arctic, operating from tiny detachments at Churchill, Yellowknife, Resolute Bay, and other remote places. Detachment life was most informal. Air and groundcrews shared common messing facilities with few, if any, military rules and regulations.

Late one night I came across Colin in the mess kitchen. He was alone, cooking up a batch of french fries and sorting through a great pile of box tops.

"What are you doing?" I asked, as he merrily sawed the top off a large cornflakes box with a bread knife.

"Just collecting these tops."

"Box tops? What for?" I questioned.

"Two hundred and fifty box tops and I can get a complete set of flatwear. It's only silver plate but the pattern looks quite nice. Don't you think?" He pushed the illustrated box of cornflakes across the table so that I could see the offer.

"How many have you collected?"

"I need ten more to get the whole set."

"For God's sake!" I was flabbergasted. "Where did you get them all? You mean you've eaten all those cornflakes?"

"No, I don't like cornflakes." He pointed to the food storage room that led off the kitchen." I got them in there."

I walked into the shelf-lined room and discovered row upon row of cereal boxes all staring at me from their open tops.

Colin had a dream of retiring to England when his RCAF days were over. He held on to the idea for a long time. It wasn't until ten years

75

after leaving England that he had a chance to visit his home town of London, and the visit destroyed his dream. He told me about it on his return to Canada.

"England has changed so much," he informed me sadly.

"How do you mean?" I asked.

"Well, I don't believe I'd ever felt more excited in my life than when I landed in London. I couldn't wait to explore my old haunts and to see my relatives. Remember I had been away ten years and I felt I was returning home. I took a cab and rushed to my aunt's house which was close to the airport.

"After knocking on her door for about five minutes I began to think there was no one home, yet I could hear the television clearly. Finally, I opened the door and walked in dragging my suitcase. The family were gathered around the television in the living room. No one got up to greet me as I stood there – the conquering hero, returning full of news about Canada and most anxious to tell my tales.

"'Oh, it's Colin.' (I think it was my uncle who said that.) 'Here, have a seat. We're watching our favourite program. You'll simply love it.'"

"Must have been disappointing," I sympathized.

"It didn't stop there. The next day I strolled around to my favourite pub to look up former friends and catch up on the news. I went to the bar, feeling delighted to be back and eager to tell one and all everything about Canada. I was standing at the end of the bar trying to catch the bartender's eye. I was feeling so pleased to be back where I had spent so many wonderful hours that at first I didn't realize I was being ignored. Finally it registered and I called for a pint of mild and bitter. 'Round to the front of the bar, if you want to be served,' the bartender snapped.

"It was a double blow, for English pubs had always enthralled me and part of my retirement plan was to own a village pub. I pictured in my dream a small English village with a greensward and Maypole and a Tudor style pub with my name across the front: *C.A. Green, Prop*. Here I would get to be a leading member of the village and reign for the rest of my life, happy and busy ....

"The most amazing thing happened after I had been so rudely greeted in my old pub. I had taken the underground to the outskirts of London to spend some time walking around, just getting the feel of England again. Suddenly I turned a corner and there, across a stretch of grass, was a Maypole – and behind it, my pub! I stood there, absolutely shocked, drinking in the scene. My name was actually across the front of the pub:

C.A. Green, Prop. For several minutes I couldn't comprehend. I'm dreaming, I told myself, I must be. My God, there it is! The Tudor pub, the Maypole, my name in large, gilt-edged letters. My dream has come true.

"When I had collected a little of my wits I hurried over. Still in a bit of a daze, I rushed into the pub. It was beautiful, all old, dark, polished wood, etched window glass, and carved corner posts set into the bar. I must have been grinning like an idiot. I know I was walking several feet off the floor as I approached the bar and the owner – who had already begun to stare at me.

"Without introducing myself I plunged into the story of how I'd just found my long-held dream. I talked about how I had been away in Canada for ten years dreaming of owning a pub just like this one, and of how now, after all that time, I'd found it. 'You'll never believe how surprised I was. It simply took my breath away when I looked up to see the pub with my name on it!' I said to him.

"I began to slow down when I realized that the owner hadn't said anything. He was just staring at me. When I stopped talking, absolute silence descended between us, and I began to get embarrassed as I realized how foolish I must have sounded, rushing in and blurting everything out in a single burst.

"'My name is the same as yours, you see,' I said. 'C.A. Green. Like on your sign.'

"Silence. He continued to stare at me. I pressed on, now deeply embarrassed. 'My first name is Colin,' I explained. I was unable to think of anything else that might make the connection and get him to understand my enthusiasm.

"Finally, the man spoke, his eyes locked on mine, his voice flat with disinterest. 'Mine's Charlie,' he said."

The trip to England removed forever any idea of retiring in that country, but Colin continued to speak nostalgically of the old, good days he had known. One of his more intriguing yarns concerned a prank he and his school chums would play on their lunch hour.

The school was located on the outskirts of London and very near the open countryside. Colin and a dozen boys would line up on a hill, Indian file, and then run down the hill at full speed onto a street lined with stores. The first store was a green grocer's, where fruit and vegetables were displayed on the sidewalk. The rules of their game called for each boy to grab an apple as they ran past the store. The last boy in the line was in the most danger of being caught by the store owner, so they took

turns being last. They played the same game each day the weather permitted. When they returned safely to the schoolyard they would exchange tales of their heroic experience as they munched their apples. The tail-ender would relate the closeness of his escape, for the green grocer always gave chase with loud yells and dire threats. They could hear him panting, his feet pounding, his very fingers scraping their backs as he chased them down the street.

Colin relived those merry chases for me so that I could actually feel the daring and excitement of the daily game.

"Never once did anyone get caught, although I was certain sometimes I wouldn't escape. I could actually feel the owner's breath on my neck. I have never run so fast in all my life! We always escaped – but only by inches."

Many years after Colin told me that story we were sitting at a roadside bar in Metz, France, enjoying the sun and wine. I remembered his tale, and because I wanted to hear it again I asked him to tell it once more.

"Didn't I ever tell you what happened?" a surprised Colin asked me.

"What do you mean?"

"About visiting the store a couple of years ago."

"No. You went to see the shopkeeper?"

"Yes. I was in London attending a military conference and had some free time, so I was wandering around as I like to do and found myself in the old neighbourhood. There, suddenly, was the store, and the scene of those long ago running battles with the fruit store owner.

"I decided, for some reason, that I wanted to meet the owner and confess that I was one of the boys who used to steal his apples. When I entered the store I wasn't sure of the reception I might get and I was slightly apprehensive. A girl of about twenty was waiting on some customers, so I waited until she was free before introducing myself. I immediately began telling her my tale and about how I now wanted to meet the owner of the store and confess.

"The girl grabbed my arm and began yelling, 'George, George, we've got one! Quick, George, here's one of those kids who used to steal our apples. Call the police!'

"Her husband rushed from the back crying, 'Hold him, hold him, I'm coming!'

"I have never felt so awkward. I nearly died with embarrassment. I didn't know whether to laugh or run or cry ....

"When things settled down they both told me that the grocer, the girl's father, had died, and had left the store to them. They were delighted to see me but sad that the store's original owner couldn't have been there.

"'Father so enjoyed those lunch hours,' the girl said. 'You know, first thing each morning, he hand polished each apple. They were special apples that he bought just for you boys. He always placed them in a box on the corner of the fruit stand, where you could reach them easily. Then he would stand behind the window, anxiously waiting and peering up the street, waiting for you to come running down the hill. He was so disappointed when it rained and you didn't come. It was the highlight of his day.

"'Of course you understand that he had to be careful not to catch you – just to always make it seem like he would.'"

*   *   *

Speaking as an old infantryman, I should like to pay tribute to a very gallant band of RAF kite-balloon pilots who manned the first observation balloons – known then as "sausages" – during the First World War.

The odds were against them all the time. In fact, they were nothing more than sitting ducks for the German fighters, who shot them up with incendiary bullets. When the pilots jumped, the imperfect parachutes of the day often failed to open. If they were lucky and the chute did open, then the Germans took pot-shots at them as they floated to earth. They did not even enjoy the privilege of firing back, as they were inadequately armed. Life was full of adventure.

I was offered an opportunity to take a trip aloft in a sausage and I accepted the chance for a bit of excitement. I'm quite sure that there would have been no attraction if it had been an order!

I duly reported at a flying field just behind the lines, not far from Armentières in northern France. At that time, owing to the limited range and relatively slow speeds of the biplanes then employed, airfields were situated much nearer to the front than they would be today. Sausages were used in great profusion by both sides in the First World War and each airfield was protected by them. Similarly, as one approached the firing line, the trenches could be traced by a double row of balloons facing each other like gargantuan lamp posts lining an aerial route.

When I arrived at my particular airfield, the first thing I did was to weigh-in, since the payload of a sausage was only 400 pounds. I turned the scales at 230 pounds, dressed in heavy field boots. As the pilot was no light weight either, I shed some of my kit to get the weight down. Further despondency was caused when it was discovered that the belt of the parachute harness would not meet on my ample figure. Eventually, I was securely lashed to the harness with a cord, which somehow did not boost my morale. Parachutes, you see, were not attached to our bodies, but were located in two wooden frames at the side of the basket – outside. Only our harness was secured to the chutes. On jumping out, the theory was that the chutes would be pulled from the frames and would open automatically.

The Sergeant on duty offered me all sorts of advice in case the sausage was attacked. He told me that, when I jumped, I would fall like a stone for 500 feet, but that I would float down from there "loike a d'isy." I tried to share his optimism. I was then handed a knife to cut the extemporized lashings when I landed.

Eventually the pilot gave the signal to let go, and up we shot. As we ascended, he regaled me with more horrors – such as the possibility that the envelope of the balloon might catch fire and fall on you as you jumped. Also, I gathered, the steel cable had been known to break, and then one was at the mercy of the wind and weather. By now I had become completely indifferent.

In about four minutes, we reached a height of 3,000 feet. Though a thirty MPH wind was blowing, the sausage was as steady as a rock. At all times, we were in telephonic contact with the ground. In the east, a trench line near Merville could be identified; and to the northwest lay Dunkirk. Calais, as well as Brighton and the Isle of Wight, were visible in the distance. As this was the first time I had left Mother Earth, it all seemed very strange to me – and I might add that I kept my glasses glued to my eyes in search of German machines. To my great relief, however, none appeared, and after a while we were wound down. As I stepped out onto *terra firma*, I thought I detected on the Sergeant's face a look of disappointment that I had not given him an opportunity to see if I would come down "loike a d'isy."

Only a few days afterwards, I learned with very great regret that my pilot had been shot down and killed while carrying out his heroic and unsung daily task.

* * *

Group Captain Sir Douglas Bader, RAF, was a famed Battle of Britain fighter pilot renowned throughout both the British and Canadian air

forces. Before his sudden death in late 1982, the legless fighter ace was a featured guest of honour at many of the ''Wartime Aircrew Reunions'' held at four or five year intervals in Winnipeg.

Bader had lost both legs in a flying accident in the pre-war RAF, and his personal struggles to regain flying status and convince the RAF of his capability became an epic chapter in a legendary life. One of the squadrons he led in the Battle of Britain was 242 squadron, which included a bunch of unruly Canadian pilots.

Escapes and recaptures while a prisoner of war made Bader well-known to the German Air Force, and one of its leaders, Adolf Galland, became his friend after the war. Bader was instrumental in getting Galland to attend the Winnipeg reunions – which at first was considered heresy of a high order by many RCAF veterans. The fact that the war was indeed over slowly made itself felt as the stretch of years lengthened. The change in attitude was helped along by Galland himself, who could tell some great yarns from a new perspective.

When, for example, Germany started producing the ME 163 and ME 262 jet fighters, quickly bringing them into operational use, the Allies had nothing that would match them. Galland, who was then head of the German Air Force, told of the shouting matches he had with Hitler as he requested to be allowed to use the new jets against the Allied bombing offensive. He quoted a face to face confrontation in which Hitler had said: ''Jet fighters keep running through your head all the time! The jet is *not* a fighter aircraft. You couldn't engage in combat with it. My doctor tells me that, in carrying out the violent movements necessary in combat, certain parts of the brain would cease to function. This aircraft is not yet fully developed – and when it is, it will not be the fighters who will get it. For you I have other aircraft, constructed in a different way conforming to proven technical experience. Say no more about this 'turbo' fighter. It is useless! I know better than you the use of aircraft!''

But the catalyst of the reunions was always Sir Douglas, who attracted famed flyers from around the world. He seemed to be the centre of everything, and nothing was ever too much trouble. Although I only met him once, I still marvel at the spirit that emanated from him. He was in Ottawa, making a stop on his way back to Britain from a visit to Winnipeg. He tried to visit as many Veterans' Hospitals as he could manage during his trips to Canada, and Cliff Chadderton, the secretary of the War Amputation Association of Canada, had arranged a small luncheon so that Sir Douglas could meet some members of the War Amps executive and the Deputy Minister of Veterans' Affairs.

At that time, the President of the War Amps happened to be a double amputee like Sir Douglas, and as the luncheon wore down, talk turned to the various new makes of artificial limbs coming on the market. Mild disagreements ensued over which country was producing the best limbs, and I remember that no one thought the Canadian varieties were any good. Sir Douglas seemed to opt for the English legs he was wearing, while Cliff Chadderton and his group were high on German manufactured limbs. For demonstration purposes, Bader and the President climbed upon chairs and rolled their pant legs up above their knees. Chadderton, with only one leg shot off, was not included in this "show and tell" skit.

There (without a camera in the room!) stood two men on tin limbs, laughing and joking about their "legs." Bader's would not permit his ankles to rotate, and I remember that, after all, he was quite impressed with the new type of leg which the President was wearing – one which articulated at the ankle.

"Good God, man, that's just what I need!" cried Bader. "They'd be absolutely marvellous for golfing. I find my spikes dig in and tend to pull me over."

*   *   *

Father Norman Gallagher was one of those RCAF padres who served in wartime and continued serving in the peacetime air force. Gallagher was a Roman Catholic, and perhaps his best friend was Bill Rodgers, an Anglican padre. Their churches often stood side by side on many RCAF bases in Canada and overseas.

One day, a terrible windstorm hit the base at Grostenquin, France, and took the roof completely off the Catholic church. Meanwhile, Rodgers' Anglican church standing alongside was untouched.

"That," said Gallagher, "proves God is a Protestant."

Norman Gallagher went on to become a Bishop later in life, and was serving as Bishop of Thunderbay, Ontario, at the time of his death. He was revered throughout the RCAF for his many attributes – not the least of which was his humour.

The story that follows is one he wrote for *The Roundel* magazine. It is an indication of the measure of the man.

Many years ago, an antique dealer in Strasbourg, Germany, drove his cart up to the Lutheran Church of St. Peter's and stopped there. He climbed down, tied his horse to a metal ring protruding from the brick wall, walked around to the side, and rang the bell of the caretaker's house. The door opened and a voice queried, "*Ja?*"

"I have come for the windows," said the dealer.

Presently, the dealer climbed back up on his seat and cracked his whip. When the horse and cart lumbered away down the cobblestone road, it was carrying several boxes of stained glass windows. It crossed the Place Kleber and plodded up to the Cathedral Square with its quaint Alsatian type buildings that surrounded and offset the majestic Strasbourg Cathedral. Eventually, the wagon halted in front of the antique shop which faced the west door of the Cathedral. While his young daughter watched, the dealer carried in the boxes containing the window sections and placed them at the back of the store room.

These events took place in 1900, when Strasbourg was in the thirtieth year of its annexation by Bismarck's Germany. Through two world conflicts, a depression, and an occupation, the windows lay unpacked in the crates in which they came. Covered with dust they were ignored and forgotten … almost.

The incident that resurrected them was an accident. My job in Europe was to set up the Roman Catholic Chaplaincy Services. In July 1954, I moved to No. 4 Wing to open that base's chapel. It was a splendid, church-like structure, complete with pews and a stone pulpit that had a wrought-iron banistered staircase leading up to it. The communion rail was a slab of polished stone on designed iron, and a fringe of the same metalwork latticed and surrounded the main altar. Near the front there were, on either side, two fourteen foot windows, both three feet wide. They formed natural frames for stained glass. It was this thought that sent me out on my hunt and, in due course, brought me to the little antique shop.

The daughter of the now dead dealer served me. She was a stout woman of well over sixty, a widow, with one son. I told her of my need and she smiled, explaining that this was not a shop that sold religious articles. Then:

"But just a moment," she added. "I had almost forgotten. We have something at the back of the shop that has been there for many years. It is stained glass, but I am afraid it is in a state of poor repair."

Moments later, she was shoving aside small pillars of Carrara marble, lifting oriental lamps carefully to safety, and straining at a large, highly-polished buffet of chequered inlay. Behind all this I spied some dusty wooden boxes, containing bundles wrapped in old German newspapers yellow with age. The first square unwrapped was a magnificent head of Christ in startling vivid colour.

Convinced that this was a find in a million I rallied my Scotch instincts and tried to look indifferent as I asked the price. Alsatians drive a hard bargain, and my heart stood still as the old lady searched my face for the slightest indication that I was anxious to buy.

"Eighty thousand?"

This was roughly two hundred and forty dollars. I nearly kissed her but long months of dealing with the Europeans had taught me restraint. To have accepted immediately or anxiously would have entailed the addition of taxes, plus service. I met her silence with silence.

"Of course, if you handle the transportation yourself, I could reduce the price to seventy-five thousand."

I reached for my wallet, made a deposit, and promised to be back. Two days later, with the whole-hearted approval and assistance of all concerned on the station, the two windows were brought in triumph to the chapel. By a rare coincidence they were almost a perfect fit for the space available.

The windows, made in Munich in 1870, were taken to the Roman Catholic Church of St. Pierre le Jeune, Strasbourg. This city (then in Germany but now in France), was to see considerable religious dissention. Claims to churches became disputes between the evenly divided numbers of Roman Catholics and Lutherans. The case of St. Pierre was forwarded to the Kaiser in Berlin. His decision came back, awarding the church to the Lutherans – and the windows were immediately removed. This occurred in 1900. It seems strange that it remained for a group of Canadians to bring them back to Germany, where they had been produced, and to install them once more in a Roman Catholic edifice.

Contributions from officers and airmen alike soon paid for them and now, once more, the light shines softly through them where they stand in No. 4 Wing's chapel at Baden-Solingen, dedicated to the cause of peace.

*   *   *

I was convinced that navigators could be placed in one of two categories: supreme optimist or supreme pessimist. I considered myself to be in the former group. However, the condition never did seem to eliminate the fear that I would forget something, or make a mistake that would cause discomfort or embarrassment (or both). On our squadron were two

86

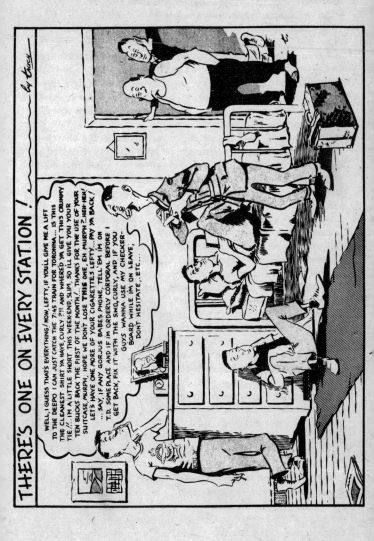

navigators who were prime examples of the two types.

Gordon considered navigation only slightly more complicated than simple addition and subtraction. With loop bearings, astro fixes, good map reading, dead reckoning, and finally the advent of "Gee" (the first radar navigation aid), he claimed there was no possible reason to get lost.

One cardinal rule for all navigators was to check the Gee system before takeoff and do whatever possible to ensure that it was operational. Most of us felt a substantial relief when the screen lit up. Gordon considered this radar aid an unnecessary benefit.

One night, as his pilot circled over the airfield and over a solid cloud base, awaiting the appointed time to set course, Gordon switched on his Gee box. No joy. The screen refused to light up. Unperturbed, Gordon got out his sextant and took two star shots. He plotted them and was astonished to find that a *tremendous wind* had pushed the aircraft over the Irish Sea – a considerable distance from base.

Undismayed, he set course from this surprising position to follow the route to the target, which was Frankfurt. He continued taking star shots to correct his position but soon discovered a serious deficiency in his sextant. His plotted positions were not feasible.

After seven hours of flying the crew had not spotted any activity. They saw no target, dropped no bombs. Fearful of running out of gas they descended below cloud to identify a position, and discovered that they were over Land's End on the southern tip of England, some 200 miles from their dead reckoning position. They landed at a nearby airfield to refuel and came merrily back to base. Gordon had proved his point! How could anybody get lost – or stay lost?

It was shortly after this episode that Gordon and his crew were shot down and killed.

Eddy represented the other side of the coin. He was the supreme pessimist. During our training courses Eddy would claim that every new course was a step closer to disaster. He strove mightily to excel in navigation so as to postpone the evil day (or night).

Strangely, his pessimism had no effect on his *esprit de corps*. Doom was inevitable – so let's live it up in the meantime!

Eddy went on to complete two tours of operations and survive the war.

* * *

There are gardeners who have green thumbs and musicians who have only to sit down at a piano for its tone to become sweeter. There have been air force navigators, too, who have been blessed with the same mysterious blend of judgement, skill, and knowledge – helped out, perhaps, with a dash of homing pigeon blood. Among their number possibly no one had it in a greater degree than Flight Lieutenant A.W. Batchelor, DFC.

His Christian names were Alexander William, but nobody ever called him anything but "Batch." He was quite tall, rather weedy, undistinguished of feature, and he had an unsoldierly slack-limbed bearing which resulted from a lack of physical co-ordination that rendered him totally incapable even of catching a ball. Possibly his most noticeable characteristic was the evil-smelling pipe that he carried with him everywhere.

He was born in Victoria, British Columbia, in 1920. In 1939, just before the war broke out, he went to England to join the RAF as a ground tradesman. His first job, and the one he always maintained was the best he ever had, was taking charge of the tea urn in an airmen's mess. Early in 1940, however, Batch was given the opportunity to remuster to aircrew and he began his training as an observer.

He took his training in Ansons, using four-miles-to-the-inch maps – a scale so large that the student navigator scarcely had time to unfold a sheet before even the slow progress of an Anson had taken him on to the next one. As a result, the inside of the aircraft very quickly became littered with map sheets.

After he had graduated as a Sergeant, with his bright new "Flying O" on his chest, he was sent to a Whitley squadron. The Whitley was an ancient monoplane that looked as if it was made from two-by-fours. Its turn of speed was such that on one occasion when Batch saw an Anson approaching, he had his pilot alter his heading by ninety degrees so that the Anson would not see how slow he was.

His first operational trip was over Germany. It was made in company with a Squadron Leader, an astronomical rank in those days. Batch navigated the aircraft to the last leg before the final run-in, and then went into the nose of the Whitley to check the bomb sight. On and on they flew, Batch desperately searching his topographical maps and the ground for something that looked familiar. Nothing appeared – until suddenly lights showed up ahead of them.

Now, whatever else one might see in Germany during the war, street lights were not among them. Batch told the pilot to steer due west until the situation cleared up a little, and they turned back towards the darkness. A flak battery obligingly fired at them and Batch dropped his bombs on it. They kept on, with the fuel in the tanks dropping lower and lower. As the continent faded away behind them, Batch and his crew checked their Mae Wests in preparation for the inevitable ditching. Then, unexpectedly, the English coast showed up and they landed at the first airfield they saw. As they turned off the runway, both engines stopped for lack of fuel.

"I don't know what was wrong with that last course I gave you before we reached the target, sir," Batch said. "Zero-sixty seemed pretty good to me."

"Zero-sixty?" the pilot exclaimed. "I thought you said One-sixty!" Then he grinned and stuck out his hand. "Wizard trip! Wizard trip! It was my fourth. On the first three I was shot down."

Navigation in those days was a very approximate business. The aircraft seldom had the ceiling to climb above the clouds, and quite often they flew to the point where dead reckoning indicated that the target should be, dropped their bombs at their Estimated Time of Arrival, (ETA), and came back again, all without benefit of any navigational fixes whatever. Needless to say the results were usually terrible, but it was on one such trip that Batch demonstrated his uncanny sense of direction.

Returning from a raid during which he had no information at all other than two radio direction-finding position lines, he received a diversion to another base. He made the course correction and then, prompted by some inner voice, gave the order for another five degrees to starboard. The course brought the aircraft right over the station. Drawing to an inside straight is child's play compared to that!

Halfway through his tour he was sent to Africa, to fly with the Wellingtons of the Desert Air Force. Before he left, he had his teeth checked over by a service dentist, who pointed out that he needed quite a lot of work done. Since it would be painful, and since Batch was aircrew and would probably be killed anyway, all the work would be wasted.

"Fair enough," said Batch, and left. When he came back from the Middle East, he could pull teeth out with his fingers.

In Africa he operated for a year against Rommel's forces, living in tents which he shared with uncounted flies and other insects, and eating bully beef mixed with sand. His method of operation in those cloudless latitudes was to read off from his astrograph the altitude of Polaris and then home down the position line, altering five degrees at a time until he got the star where he wanted it in the bubble of his sextant; (which, incidentally, was so clogged with sand that it would take only single shots). Theoretically, his method is analogous to stepping into the batter's box and expecting to get a home run each time. It is quite indefensible. For Batch it worked fine.

He came back to England where he did an instructional tour at a bomber Operational Training Unit at Pershore. When that was over he went back on operations with a Mosquito Pathfinder squadron. Many of his trips with it were for the purpose of target marking by OBOE, a radio aid that involved flying on a steady heading over some enemy objective. In his spare time he bombed Berlin.

On one occasion he had a close brush with death. Taking off with a 4,000 pound bomb aboard, a young Flight Sergeant pilot lost control of the Mosquito and headed for the hangars. Batch hopped out of his seat, reached over the pilot's shoulders, and pulled the aircraft off the ground. It thundered over the hangars with inches to spare. Batch relinquished control to the pilot and they went on and bombed Berlin.

When the war ended, Batch was a Squadron Leader with a Distinguished Flying Cross and Bar. He left the RAF and returned to Victoria. Then, in 1947, he joined the RCAF, in which he was given the rank of Flying Officer. After a short stint in the non-public accounts office at Patricia Bay, he was posted to the Communications Flight at Edmonton. Here he was introduced to the glories of Arctic navigation.

In the Arctic, Batch was in his element. Scorning the special log form devised for gyro-navigation, he entered in his main log all the extra work required by the technique of steering without a magnetic compass. He was well-equipped, having a thirty-year-old wrist watch with a stop mechanism registering half seconds. This he used to time the passage of objects through a drift recorder in order to obtain groundspeeds. The astronomical navigation tables used by most of the rest of the air force were too simple for him. He preferred a copy of Ageton's Tables, which he carried in his back pocket. Likewise beneath him was the measuring of tracks and distances on a map. He calculated them from his Ageton.

He flew all over the Arctic one summer with Squadron Leader Bill Clark, who was not noted as a particularly easy man to please. The latter's comment on his navigator was simple: "The best in the business."

On one trip from Churchill to Ottawa, the only map Batch had was a used meteorological chart that reached only halfway to Ottawa. He climbed over the bags of potatoes and tool boxes in the Canso and set to work. Having previously worked out his great circle track and distance by Ageton's Tables, he converted them to rhumb line values by adding five degrees to one and twenty miles to the other. Then, calculating the wind by drifts and groundspeeds obtained with the help of his ancient stop watch, he kept a track-plot. After a couple of hours he ran into cloud and seized the opportunity to smoke his pipe. He kept one eye open, however, and when the cloud type changed, he noted the time in order to decide when to stop using the last wind and to start using the new one he would get when the ground was visible.

Since the meteorological chart did not cover the whole distance to Ottawa, Batch took a piece of chalk and drew a line on the side of the aircraft to represent the distance. Every twenty minutes he calculated how far he had gone and, with a nail, scratched out part of the line. Then, with a pencil (he always broke his pencils in half so he would have twice as many) he entered up his log.

When his ETA was up he should have been, according to his calculations, over the airport. He wasn't. He was over the Parliament Buildings. In the bar that night, an American officer with him on that trip, said: "We're here, because we're drinking – but I still don't believe it."

It was while he was in Edmonton that he entered a room in which one of his fellow navigators was taking practice sights on the sun with his sextant. Batch lit his pipe and stood the burned match on the window sill. From the length of the shadow he estimated the altitude of the sun. When he worked out his "sight," his position line was two miles closer than the one the other man had measured with his sextant.

In 1949 he went to Summerside to take the Staff Navigation Instructor's Course. Flying with another navigator he asked for a pinpoint. The weather was foggy and all the information he could be given was that he had just crossed a coastline. He used this as a pinpoint by estimating where he had crossed the coast; then he found a wind at 9,000 feet, estimated what it would be at 4,000 feet, and flew directly over base perfectly on ETA.

In 1951 Batch was sent to England on an exchange posting. Early in the following year he decided to take a flight that was going to Gibraltar, so that he could buy his wife some stockings. Two cadets were navigating. The aircraft hit a mountain in France and all on board were killed.

Batch, the best natural navigator I ever knew, lies buried in a French churchyard.

Per Ardua Ad Astra

We were in bed when we were told: "Briefing in twenty minutes." We got out of bed in a real hurry and rushed off to briefing. This would be our first operational trip! The target was Frankfurt, and it was to be a maximum effort.

It was a rush to get ready for the unexpected trip. None of the crew felt ready for our first op. I remember putting soap, toothpaste, toilet paper, and canned goods inside my flying suit. If I had to bail out I was determined to be ready for anything.

The takeoff seemed to last forever, but finally the heavily loaded Lancaster staggered off and our navigator hollered over the intercom, "Frankfurt, here we come!"

As we climbed on track we could see a great swarm of Lancasters and Halifaxes flying on all sides of us. It gave us confidence. I put my guns in the front turret to fire and fused my bombs. Soon it became dark and we could see no other planes. But we knew they were beside us.

"Corkscrew left!" came the frightened voice of the rear gunner.

"Eh?" said the pilot.

"It's all right. The fighter has gone by now."

I thought to myself: *Not only do I have a slow-witted pilot – but blind gunners! How are we ever going to survive?* But we did survive that night and all the other nights on our tour of ops.

* * *

"I'll never fly again" was an expression I remember using very often. *Please God, just get us home in one piece and I'll never fly again.*

It was the usual dash to be in time for flying supper and briefing. We took off with a 4,000 pound cookie headed for Darmstadt just south of Frankfurt. We saw nothing but darkness till we reached that horrible great belt of searchlights on the Rhine.

The Germans shot up two or three scarecrows in front of us which worried me for a moment. Then the searchlights played about with us. One aircraft was coned on our right and had flak bursting all around him. Then *we* got coned when we were halfway through the searchlight belt. Flak was hammered at us.

"Turn to starboard skipper!" the rear gunner yelled.

We seemed to get away from the flak for a moment, and then it came again. We could hear it hitting the aircraft and it sounded like someone throwing stones against the kite. I couldn't see much of it except one

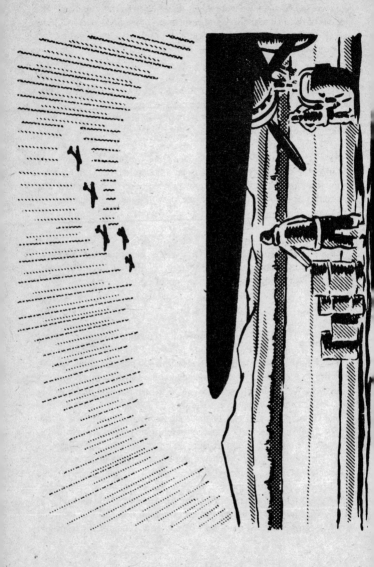

great flash in front of me and a cloud of dirty black smoke. Apparently it was bursting all around us like that. Sudden, blinding flashes of light and then black patches of smoke. I grabbed for my chute and fastened it on. I saw the engineer grab for his and the navigator, on seeing the engineer, did the same thing. We screamed at the skipper to weave.

Suddenly, the mid-upper gunner yelled over the intercom, "I've been hit. I've got some of it in my eye. I'm half blind!" A piece of shell had gone through his perspex just missing his head by inches. The rear gunner added, "I've been hit, too. My turret is awfully sluggish." The navigator piped in with, "My instruments won't work, now." Then the mid-upper gunner said, "I'm not sure whether this is blood or sweat running down my face." It was sweat.

We got through the searchlight belt and headed in for the target. We were to bomb the red markers. The run-in seemed to take hours. The pilot kept calling me, "Bomb doors open?" and I'd reply, "No, no, not yet."

The whole fucking sky was on fire. The city was completely covered by one terrible blaze. Smoke, thick brown clouds of it, floated around the whole area. Very concentrated. When the crew heard the bombs go they all sighed, "Thank God for that!"

We turned and headed home. Fighters shot tracers across the skies. We saw kites go down. There were still the bloody searchlights to pass through again .... We flew all over the sky dodging them. *So help me*, I kept saying to myself, *I'll never, never fly again. Please God, get me back home safe tonight and I'll never fly again. Just once more, please, please.*

Well, we made it through the searchlights, but fighters appeared to chase us most of the way back. Finally we got over England. It was then that the rear gunner said: "Anyone who wasn't scared tonight is telling a lie."

"This must be your first stiff trip," the pilot said to him. "How do you like it?"

We got home safely, thank God, but not before landing at the wrong airfield by mistake. Then we had to take off and fly to our own field, and while we were taxiing around the perimeter track we saw a kite approaching us as it was trying to land. We all panicked, though we were on the runway.

"Full power!" cried the pilot to the engineer.

We shot across the grass and, because our brakes weren't any too good, ended up against a hedge. The wireless operator said, "One more trip like this and I'm going LMF."*

I got to bed at 5:30 feeling very tired.

*   *   *

We took off with twelve 1,000 pound bombs and some cans of incendiaries. Our target was Aachen just over the French border. It was a short trip, but I sensed trouble even before we started. I think I bombed that target more accurately than any other.

On our return I could see many battles going on in the sky. Looking downwards once I saw a Lancaster firing straight back at something. Fighter flares were being dropped all over the place. We were flying along nice and steady when suddenly *zing-zing*. I felt bullets hit right below where I was lying in the nose and saw tracers shoot out ahead of us. We were all paralyzed with fear and shock for a moment. As our pilot started to shove the nose down I yelled at him to "Dive! Dive like crazy!"

When our rear gunner said that the attack seemed to be over, our pilot pulled the Lancaster up and we wove a good part of the way home. The engineer advised we should feather the port inner engine, and we flew on three engines the rest of the way. "You wouldn't know there was a thing wrong with the aircraft," the pilot said, "although the elevator is a little sluggish."

"What did you fire at?" the navigator asked the rear gunner.

"I fired at the blinding flash or red tracer bullets. It all happened so fast I didn't see the fighter at all."

"I couldn't see the fighter, either," the mid-upper gunner volunteered.

Over base we circled many times but couldn't raise the control tower, so we fired a pistol flare before coming in for our landing. The hydraulics were gone so we had to hand pump the flaps and wheels down. As we slowed to a stop, a blown left tire skidded us around to the left. I jumped out to see the damage. The Lanc was quite a mess. The upper part of the port inner nacelle was shot clean away. A cannon shell had gone clear through our radiator. The upper surface of the leading edge of the wing had been pulled upwards, bolts and all. Bullets or splinters had hit the side and bottom of my bomb-aimer's compartment. Our left tire was shot; and the port elevator was ripped apart.

*Lack of Moral Fibre.

"Ha, ha, you missed us, you bastard!" we yelled towards Germany – just as the Wing Commander arrived to inspect the damage.

He didn't see the humour of it. "It was a real close call," he said.

* * *

I found some operational briefings so nerve wracking that I always broke out laughing. This was a common thing, I noticed. The first time No. 5 Group was to do a daylight raid, the target selected was Strasbourg. It seemed a ridiculous target after all the Ruhr cities and Berlin, and for some reason we all howled with laughter. When we were told that it would be a very early morning takeoff, a guy said, "I think I'll sleep in." The remark brought the house down.

* * *

Somehow we had inherited an old gramophone and one, only one, record. We would crank the machine to full power and play the scratchy recording of Harry Horlick's, "The Count of Luxembourg" on one side and "Eva" on the other. It was our "Lili Marlene" of the Second World War. We never tired of playing it.

* * *

My thirteenth op was a real hairy one. I was the bomb aimer lying prone in the nose of the famous Lancaster heavy bomber. My compartment had a plastic bubble nose and, so that I could see everything that went on ahead or below, part of the floor was perspex as well. I often wished I couldn't see anything.

The briefing disclosed that the target was a flying bomb storage depot just north of Paris. This was a heavily defended area with many German night fighters – and we were to bomb at 16,000 feet in the light of a full moon. The pilot was an Australian and so was the wireless operator. The mid-upper gunner, like myself, was Canadian, while the navigator, rear gunner, and flight engineer were RAF blokes.

We took off with our load tucked neatly under us, and the yellow moon shining brilliantly down. As we approached London we got a picture I don't think I can ever forget. We could see Lancasters above, below, and all around us, all flying in the same direction. Ahead we could see sprays of flak shooting up from the city, which had about

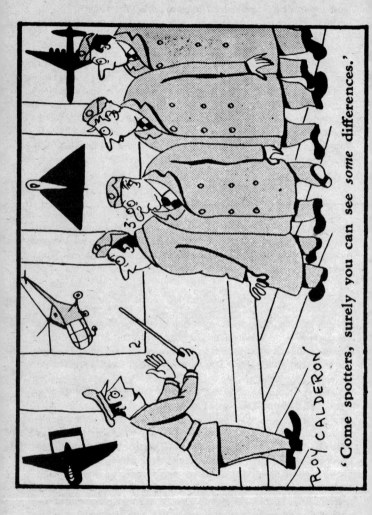

'Come spotters, surely you can see *some* differences.'

ROY CALDERON

eight-tenths cloud. They were shooting at buzz bombs, the pilotless planes the Germans launched from the European coast. As I watched the flak I reminded myself not to go on leave to London anymore. It was too damned dangerous!

We flew on across the Channel till we reached the French coast. There we met some forty searchlights waving aimlessly, searching for the bombers. They stretched unevenly on our course some twenty-five miles inland. Although we were picked up three or four times, we managed to weave out of them.

Then, some sixty miles from Paris, the fight began. Fighters started searching for us, and in the moonlight we were easy to find. We saw a Lancaster hit the deck and burst into flames right in front of us. A thin layer of patchy cloud soon covered up the glow, and as we flew closer to it we saw a single parachute floating slowly to earth.

We weren't certain whether the aircraft in the distance were fighters or not, but the pilot wove around until we lost them. A combat was going on just off to our starboard, streams of tracer flying from a night fighter. The fire was returned by the Lancaster. Another kite was on fire on our port. You could see two bright white glows, like two engines on fire, glide slowly to earth and then explode as they hit the deck. You could see a long, long way around you. It was such a brilliant, moon-lit night!

I kept looking at my watch, but the minutes seemed to take hours to pass. There were still another eight minutes to go on this particular leg. *This is damn serious*, I thought to myself. *We'll never get there without being attacked. Maybe it would be safer to bail out now, while everything is okay ....*

Yet another combat began over on our port bow. Yet another Lancaster was on fire. This was fucking suicide! We kept on weaving and searching. An ME 210 flew fast across our nose, or maybe it was a Mosquito. I couldn't tell. At last, we saw the flares being dropped and the markers going down. "We're over Paris!" I called to the skipper. "I can see a built-up area."

In front of us, black puffs of exploding flak appeared. Weaving constantly, we turned and headed for the target. The markers were well placed and brilliantly lit, and there was no cloud – so we pranged the target without much trouble. It was such a relief to get rid of the bombs, a relief too wonderful to describe. Now: if we could only sneak home without being attacked! If we did, it seemed to me that we would be the only ones to manage it. Even now, three combats were going on right beside us. One fighter was shooting away with everything he had at a Lanc. As the two planes turned to go under us the fighter kept on firing, and I could see the tracer, great white balls of fire flashing through the air. Everything – the Lancaster, the flashes of tracer, and the fighter – went right under our kite and over to the starboard side.

At that moment, the gunners saw a JU 88 come across below us from behind. The mid-upper gunner told us exactly where it was. In a calm and unexcited voice he said, "It's crossing beneath us … it's right under us now … now it's on the other side …. Better dive port, skipper!"

We dove off to port and the rear gunner fired a great long burst. As his tracer bullets went all around the plane, we heard him yell, "I hit it! I hit it!" Unfortunately, he couldn't have hit it, for the JU 88 throttled back and did a climbing turn after us. And that was when the ammunition belts jammed. We were defenceless.

"He's firing at us, skipper. Dive starboard!"

We dove starboard in a hell of a manoeuvre, climbed up again, dove again.

"He's coming in again, skipper, and he's firing!"

We dove to port, and a cannon shell hit us, putting a hole in one of our petrol tanks and wrecking the hydraulic system. Up, down, and around we went, fighting for our lives.

"We're losing petrol, skipper," called the engineer.

"Get down into those clouds below," a gunner cried, immediately afterwards.

We did. As the fighter closed in and let loose another burst the skipper slammed the Lancaster into one hell of a dive. I got stuck to the top of my compartment, and right there with me were my maps, parachute, papers, and pencils. The navigator shot up from his seat along with all his charts, his compass, and his protractor and computer. The wireless operator lost all his Verey cartridges out of his flight bag (and he never did find them). The Elsan, our chemical toilet, spilled all over the rear of the Lanc. We dived from 14,000 to 6,000 feet in what seemed like seconds, and when the pilot pulled out I was sick. We pulled out at 400 miles an hour. The skipper said later that he never thought the wings would stay on.

But were we safe? No. "He's still on our tail, skip," shouted the rear gunner. "Dive some more!"

We were all scared. The pilot rolled over in a dive to starboard as the mid-upper gunner directed him. There were clouds at 5,000 feet – but they were thin layers which were almost transparent, and we flew right through them. The rear gunner's instructions kept coming: "He's clos-ing in .... Keep diving .... Don't stop .... He's still right behind us ...."

Tracers came in from the port and seemed to circle towards us. When they got to about ten feet from me, we apparently swerved just in time to escape. I grabbed my parachute and strapped it on. In my panic I inflated my Mae West life jacket by mistake and it filled up like a balloon, tightening my parachute harness something horrible.

"Dive port, skipper ... no, no, starboard, quick!"

We flew around in a sharp circle as tracers came under our starboard wing and hit our tail section.

"We're going the wrong way!" the navigator yelled. "We're heading back to where we came from!"

"Well, Jesus, I can't help that!" roared the pilot. We flew into more cloud. "You okay, bomb aimer?" the skipper went on, after a moment. "I was sure you got hit that last time."

"No, I'm okay," I said. "It just missed me. But I do feel awfully sick."

"I *have* been sick," the navigator reported.

The skipper turned us on to our proper course, and it wasn't long before we were being attacked again. More tracer streamed by us from the starboard side. I kept saying to myself that if I ever got home, so help me, I'd never fly again. I would go LMF. I would admit that I was yellow. We hadn't a dog's chance of getting away. What would it feel like, I wondered, to be hit by bullets or cannon shells, or to be blown up in the sky, as I had seen so many other Lancs do this night? I was certain that every one of the crew had completely given up all hope of getting home. At least we all said so afterwards.

The agony went on. I had one hand on the emergency escape hatch, ready to bail out at a moment's notice. I was sick three times but couldn't cough anything up. I lay there suffering and waiting for the end. We all waited for the end.

By now we were down to 2,000 feet and the gunners could still see the JU 88. It came in so close, 150 yards, that the engineer could see the letter "S" on its nose and the Iron Crosses on its wings. Whenever the gunners couldn't catch sight of the JU 88 through the cloud, they had to judge where it was from the tracer being fired at us. They were often uncertain which way the skipper should turn to get away from the con-tinual bursts of fire.

For a moment, just as we reached the coast of the North Sea, we thought we had lost the fighter. We raced across the coast at 2,000 feet with throttles fully open. The flak guns sent up a dreadful spray of light flak and it was probably the most horrible moment of our fight for life. The wall of searchlights and the flak hosing up seemed to doom us. We could *never* fly through it.

Suddenly, the impossible happened. The searchlights moved off and the firing from the ground stopped. We figured out later that they were giving the JU 88 a chance to get us. And he was still trying. My heart almost stopped beating as the rear gunner yelled, ''He's firing again, skipper! Weave like buggery!''

Jesus! We couldn't manoeuvre at this height. And if we got shot down now we wouldn't have time to bail out. We would go straight into the sea and blow to pieces. Definitely, we'd had it.

''How far to the English coast, navigator?'' asked the pilot. ''About 100 miles,'' came the answer. Although the cloud was too thin and too spotty to hide us we continued to try and play hide and seek with the fighter. And finally the end came. A couple of flak ships anchored off-shore opened up at us. They missed as we wove out of the way – but the firing seemed to be a signal to the JU 88. We lost him. Or maybe he was out of ammunition.

When another aircraft was spotted on our port there were some anxious moments before it was identified as another Lancaster. It flew closer and stayed alongside for a while. We discovered, when we got home, that this Lanc had seen us being attacked all the way. Knowing that we were defenceless it had tried to come to our rescue.

We climbed to 10,000 feet. The engineer reported loss of petrol, but we were now only forty-five miles from England. Each minute I felt a lot safer, and when we saw the English coastline and the searchlights, tears of joy came to my eyes. I was still feeling awfully sick, though. The navigator was being *very* sick.

We arrived over our base only to be told to divert to Spilsby. Once more we assumed our crash positions for landing, for we weren't sure of the damage to our Lanc. We used emergency air to shove our wheels and flaps down and we landed quite easily. Not that I wasn't worried.

At last we got out of the Lanc and touched the good old earth. I don't think I have ever felt so relieved in all my life! ''I feel like bending down and kissing the ground,'' I said – and the mid-upper gunner promptly did just that. To us it wasn't silly or dramatic; we had suffered the greatest shocks of our lives. This trip was worse than all the trips I had done put together.

Damage to the aircraft was widespread. I kept a piece of our tail as a souvenir.

* * *

Our crew had developed a technique of separating ourselves from the herd at 20,000 feet by taking off power, lowering our wheels and flaps, opening the bomb doors, and executing a ''falling leaf'' drop down to about 2,000 feet. Right over the target. This got us out of a hell of a lot of trouble: Jerry assumed we were dead and concentrated on the guys away above us.

After doing a touch-and-go on the target we would tuck up our under-things and quickly buzz off. This worked wonderfully for about twelve raids. But then, during a bombing raid on Essen, it all hit the fan.

I had been controlling the air gunners' fire and giving intelligence to the skipper from the astrodome position, which was the wireless oper-ator's job in our crew. The target was a brilliantly-lit thing filled with flashing lights of every hue – not the least of which were the bursts of light ack-ack fire from the hilltops along the river, shooting *down* on us! We were skipping over the barges and bridges on the Rhine River when one of the shells hit. Or was it a dozen all at once?

I was enveloped in smoke and cordite and a zinger sailed through the armour plating which was protecting me. My left leg suddenly became paralyzed. No pain. There was sweat on my brow as I began to reel from the heart-pounding thrill of it all. Calming down, I asked the navi-gator to come and help me as I flaked out on the rest bed. In the utter black of the cabin with only the blue-paper-covered ''torch'' to guide him, he felt around the leg that we both thought had been shot. Just above the knee of the old canvas and leather flying boot there seemed to be a hell of a lot of seepage. In the blue light we both figured I was going to be a basket case.

The navigator shot me full of morphine from the first aid kit, and put on a field bandage at the point where it appeared that most of the blood was flowing. I soon fell asleep from the morphine, waking up only as they were moving me from the aircraft into an ambulance.

I accepted the ride to the hospital, but when I got inside the hospital I protested that I was okay. I tried to get up. The medical officer asked me how I felt and I said things would be better if they would let me walk. I got out from under the grey blanket and placed both feet firmly on the floor. Woozy at first, I marched around a little. Then we all began looking for the blood.

I sure had a boot full of it. It began to squish as I walked around in the operating room. But we soon all realized that I was a victim of battle shock and that there wasn't any blood at all. I had merely pissed in my boot!

*　　*　　*

One night our squadron of Wellingtons was detailed to bomb an airfield just north of Rome. We were stationed in North Africa with 425 squadron, and had the usual uneventful trip across the Mediterranean.

Our Wellington had been modified to carry the 4,000 pound cookie – which was a considerable feat for the venerable, two-engined Wimpy. When the bomb was released the old Wellington always jumped upwards a few hundred feet, so we could always tell when the bomb had fallen away. Of course, a check was made as soon as it was safe to do so away from the target.

Three of the squadron's Wellingtons had been selected to illuminate the target with flares, and as we began our bomb run-up the target was perfectly clear. So were the heavy flak bursts all around us. As our bomb was released the Wimpy lurched skyward as usual. The photo flash exploded and the automatic camera took a picture. Perfect! We could see all the bombs exploding on the airfield since we were only at 8,000 feet.

Five minutes after starting on the homeward leg we did our after-bombing check by opening the bomb doors and sliding the jettison bar across. There was a sudden thump and the Wimpy rose dramatically. Then a great explosion shook our aircraft as our 4,000 pounder exploded beneath us in an olive grove.

The lurching sensation over the target had obviously been caused by the heavy flak bursts. Our bomb hadn't fallen on the target after all. It was a quiet crew that flew across the Med for Africa.

At debriefing none of the crew mentioned the incident – but we were fascinated by the descriptions given by the other crews of what they had seen. They reported seeing a huge munitions dump explode south of the target. Just where we had dropped our 4,000 pounder. The next morning, when the target films were developed and the aiming points posted on the target maps, our photo was credited with a direct hit.

*　　*　　*

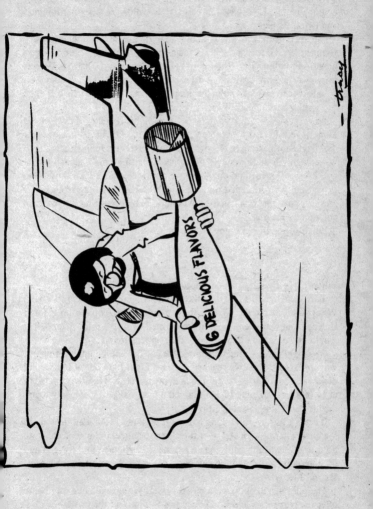

In my opinion, the most dangerous part of flying night bombing operations was the risk of a mid-air collision. I saw many of these on my tour and on one raid I witnessed three separate collisions, one over England and two over Germany.

Our own crew was hit by another Halifax over Holland. We were flying at 19,000 feet and had started a dog-leg to kill time before beginning our bombing run. The top of the fuselage near the astrodome was torn away and my instrument panel was shattered. The flight engineer, who had been on look-out in the dome, had just ducked down to change fuel cocks when the collision occurred.

As we staggered away, a mass of searchlights coned us. I dove out of them, levelling out at 8,000 feet, but we were without oxygen or heat. The frigid air blasting in through the roof caused a lot of confusion, and we suddenly found ourselves all alone over München-Gladbach where the flak guns opened up on us and we got riddled a bit. Our target was Soest, and we proceeded on to it just the same, bombing from 8,000 feet. We made it back as far as Woodbridge before we had to make an emergency landing.

Luckily, we all got home without injuries.

* * *

When I was flying as a mid-upper gunner with No. 10 squadron, we usually went out on a raid over the Cromer Light, on the Norfolk coast. We always crossed the point at about 5,000 feet, so sometimes I would ride up front with the pilot until we reached Cromer Light. After that, I would go back and climb into the mid-upper turret.

One night I was sitting up front in the cockpit enjoying myself on our way to Essen. When we reached Cromer Light I got out of the second dickey seat and started to walk back to my turret. Not realizing we were at 14,000 feet, and that I hadn't turned on any oxygen, I suddenly found the aircraft taking a sudden dive.

It wasn't the aircraft taking a dive. It was me. I rolled all the way to the back where I knocked over the Elsan chemical toilet. For about an hour or so I was out cold. When I came to, I plugged into oxygen and the intercom and called the skipper. "How much longer to the target, skip?" I asked.

The pilot just about burst a blood vessel. We were on our way home over the North Sea and I had been unconscious all the time!

* * *

We never carried waist gunners on our Liberators. If a gunner was needed, the wireless operator went back and manned a machine gun.

Once we were headed for Bangkok, and the pilot told the wireless operator to go back and man the guns. I always flew in my rear turret with the doors open over the target to make sure I could make a swift exit. On this day I happened to look back up the fuselage and there was the wireless operator lying flat on the floor. I jumped out of my turret and ran back to him. "Where are you hit?" I yelled.

The wireless operator looked at me. "I'm not hit. But if you think I'm going to put my head out that window, you're fucking well crazy!" He never saw anything in his normal crew position and he wanted no part of looking at a target.

It was on that trip, too, that the second pilot gave me a tip about putting my revolver between my legs before we started on the bomb run. This was to protect your vital parts. I did as he suggested but forgot to ask him if he took the bullets out of the gun before putting it between his legs. I found out later that he had never even thought about it.

* * *

We were on a sweep over France: twelve Spitfire IX's led by our CO, with me flying as his number two. I hadn't shot anything down, although I had tangled with ME 109's several times.

Suddenly, about 5,000 feet below but ahead of our formation and on a reciprocal course, I spotted a dozen FW 190's. I called them out to my leader. The planes were in perfect position for our bounce and my lips began drying in anticipation.

It seemed an eternity before our leader replied that he had them in sight – but then he kept on flying straight ahead. In a few seconds it would be too late! I called again and he acknowledged my call but never gave the order to attack. Fearful of missing this golden opportunity I peeled away and dove down on the German formation. Several Spitfires immediately took off after me, followed, eventually, by all the rest.

I was up-sun and in the perfect spot and I nailed two for certain before breaking off for base. If all of us had gone to the attack immediately we could have shot them all down.

Back at base, as we jubilantly exchanged stories, I expected a blast from the CO for breaking formation. But he never said a word – and to this day I wonder why.

* * *

I did my ops with No. 78 squadron as a rear gunner on Halifax bombers. One night, a crew was short a gunner so I volunteered to be tail-end Charlie for them. It was the crew's first or second mission but it was my thirteenth op. The date was December 11, 1942.

We got into some desperate trouble over France. The aircraft went into a violent tail spin, and the pilot ordered the crew to bail out. My well-rehearsed procedures for bailing out of the rear turret were as follows:

1. Point the four Browning machine guns straight aft.
2. Open turret doors with my elbows.
3. Reach inside aircraft for parachute pack.
4. Close turret doors.
5. Snap clamps on parachute onto clips on harness.
6. Disconnect intercom and oxygen.
7. Rotate turret with guns pointing starboard.
8. Open turret doors and fall out backwards.

The falling out backwards wasn't as easy as they had said it would be. I tried lifting my body out head first, but my right foot got caught in the turret. Now my parachute pack was dangling over my head, just out of reach – something to add to my panic as the Halifax hurtled down! By pulling on the strings I finally brought the pack to me, yanked the rip cord, and floated free into a silent blackness.

I was captured after landing in France, but managed to escape after two months. I dodged through the country for another four months until I finally crossed over into Spain via the Underground's Comet line.

When I returned to my base I got the shock of my life. The rest of the crew hadn't bailed out after all. They had returned safely to base on that night of December 11, 1942. While I was busy trying to escape from France they had continued flying operations and were shot down. I have never heard of them or seen them since.

One of the things that has always intrigued me about my thirteenth op is the continuing thought that all of the crew were sergeants. I was the only officer.

*   *   *

About a month after D-Day my chum, who was also a bomb aimer, was sitting with me in our favourite pub, knocking back the beer. As the evening wore on we got the fantastic idea of bailing out on purpose, the next time we did an operational flight.

This would be a "delaying" tactic we decided. The Allied armies were now advancing swiftly towards Germany, and had liberated large chunks of the continent, including Paris. If we "accidentally" bailed out over liberated territory it would take at least a month to get back to Britain. By then the war might be over and we'd still be in one piece.

So, deep into the beer, we plotted how to accomplish the trick. We decided that whoever flew next would pretend that his escape hatch had fallen out in the nose compartment and that he had fallen out with it. He would parachute to safety behind the Allied lines and be treated with all the glory and comforts of a liberator. With a little luck we could dilly-dally away the time until the armistice came. A simple, marvellous scheme.

My friend's turn came up first, since he was "on" that night .... The next morning, I was amazed to see that he was sound asleep in his bed. It was not until supper time that I was able to find out what had happened, and why he hadn't bailed out like we had planned.

"It was terrible!" he said. "We were flying over unoccupied territory and I opened up the escape hatch in the floor and jettisoned it downward. Then I attached my parachute to my harness and called the pilot over the intercom. 'Skipper, the escape hatch has blown open and I'm falling out. There's nothing anyone can do to save me .... See you!'

"But unfortunately, when I looked down through the hatch into the black, cold night, I just couldn't jump. It got so cold I had to crawl back out of the compartment. The pilot and crew just about froze to death and we had to abort the mission and return to base. Oh, Jesus, but the crew gave me hell – and most of them won't speak to me. I'll never do that again. Ever!"

How to Bend Them

Harry was quite some character. Funny thing, but I always had the impression he was English, an RAF type who had somehow wormed his way into the RCAF. Perhaps it was because he was so unflappable. Nothing ever seemed to bother him.

Prangs left him totally unruffled, and I still have a mental picture of him climbing unconcernedly from a Hally Bag he crash landed at Leeming. And then there were the landing circuits. Remember how in Yorkshire the Canadian bomber bases were so close together? The circuits almost overlapped, and guys were continually landing at the wrong base after returning from an op.

Harry seemed to do this constantly. One night, several of us had joined the circuit over Leeming and were jockeying for position. Harry was scheduled to pancake immediately ahead of our crew. We heard the instructions going to him from Teddy, our English control tower WAAF. "Turn rrright at the end of the rrrunway. Over."

Harry evidently got his Hally safely onto the runway; but after a short interval he came on the air. "Are you sure?" he asked. "There's no right turn at the end of this runway. Over."

Almost immediately the Wingco thundered in our ears. "Harry, you're on the wrong bloody airfield! Come to my office at ten hundred hours tomorrow morning."

Harry seemed destined for trouble. One night he accidentally taxied his fully loaded Halifax off the perimeter track into some deep mud. It was just off the end of the runway being used for takeoff and this blocked everyone else.

Our crew was just behind him and a dozen others were behind us, all waiting our turn to take off. Harry tried revving his engines in attempts to get free but – no luck. A message was relayed by the groundcrew, since all aircraft had to maintain radio silence, and the Wingco suddenly arrived in a jeep doing about 120 miles an hour. I got the rest of the story from Harry's engineer the next day.

Apparently, the Wingco came tearing into the aircraft and practically yanked Harry out of the pilot's seat. He then goosed hell out of the four engines, rocking the kite furiously from side to side until it struggled back onto the runway. After lining the aircraft up the Wingco got up and, still mad as hell, grabbed Harry and literally threw him into the pilot's seat.

"There. Get going. I'm not going to fly the bloody op for you, too!"

Types like Harry stood out a mile but, fortunately, there didn't seem to be many of them. Maybe that was because they were so inept they

didn't last long. Who knows. But we all liked Harry very much. He just had peculiar ways. We felt sorry when we heard he'd gone for a burton.

*   *   *

Sometimes we landed at the wrong airfield after getting landing instructions for another one. The airfields were very close together. It was really confusing after landing at a strange base because you never knew which way to turn at the end of the runway. It happened twice with our crew, and our pilot got so confused with everyone giving him so many directions that he turned and started taxiing straight back up the runway! We had to make a mad dash right off the side of the runway when the control tower shot off warning flares.

*   *   *

And then there was the pilot whose landings were so terrible he didn't know whether to declare the aircraft or the runway U/S when he bounced in.

*   *   *

Don't ever think that only a pilot loves his aircraft like a brother. I often felt like breaking into tears over an aircraft. Betsy was my particular pride and joy – I was able to get a good 3,000 revs from her at all times. Then one day, after a real hard workout, she lost a couple of hundred. We looked everywhere for them. In the cockpit, the fuselage, and even in the pilot's pockets! But still there was just 2,800 revs.

Complete with tin hat and respirator slung at the alert I worked for three hours in the middle of an open field. Finally, I found the missing 200 revs. I put all the cowlings back, wiped Betsy's face clean, and went in search of the Bowser.

And then the air raid siren went. We all dove for the nearest hole, and I watched as two JU 88's raced across the field, proceeding to plaster the place end to end. Old Betsy was in the middle of it all. Suddenly, it was all over – and there she was, a mass of twisted metal. I could have sat down and cried.

*   *   *

I wonder how many current grease monkeys realize how gratifying it is to change a set of plugs or synchronize a pair of mags in the comfort of a nice large hangar?

Riggers and fitters will appreciate how annoying it would be to have a light and battery under one arm, your mag just nicely synchronized ready to bolt up, when suddenly your tin hat drops over your eyes and blinds you. After a few curses you re-time the mags.

I can remember being balanced precariously between the V's of a Merlin fitting a new compressor to the ''A'' block when ''Wailing Winnie'' sounded. I found myself being taken for a ride as several people lifted the tail of the Spitfire and manhandled the aircraft to a safer position. I was still juggling with a splined drive and trying to get it to fit when a large camouflage net was thrown over the aircraft *and* me and the NCO was yelling: ''Don't worry, chum. As long as you stay under that net you'll be okay. Just get that fucking drive fitted!''

I went on working but found, after a bit, that the net seemed to attract Jerries instead of keeping them away. They took an intense delight in trying to blow the net, the Spit, and me right off the map. I guess they didn't know I was just a poor, underpaid, hardworking fitter .... When I got the job done I looked everywhere for the rigger to see that he did his side of it. Needless to say he was hiding behind a drum of oil, and when I asked, ''How about the compressor?'' his reply was: ''What *about* the compressor? What about my fucking neck?''

* * *

It seemed that every time we got a decent collection of tools a stray bomb would find them. It got so that a fitter's tools were a hammer and a screwdriver while a rigger's were a hide-faced hammer and a pair of pliers.

* * *

We had to be alert for German raiders on all occasions. Many a time a damned Jerry came over and caused me to drop a nut or bolt in the grass. I'd have to search for it for hours while muttering unkind things about Germans. Never a day went by without a prang of some sort – mainly due to hydraulics being shot away and undercarriages failing. As soon as the dust cleared from the crash landing we were all over the

kite. New legs and hydraulics were fitted while the aircraft still rested in the middle of the airfield.

*   *   *

There was quite a lot of time during the war when we had nothing to do but wait for our aircraft to return from a sortie. When they came in we were all over them like a swarm of bees. Some might have just limped home, in which case parts from one would be taken to service another. It became second nature to interchange engines, main-planes, oleo legs, and tail-planes. I always wondered how some of them got home.

One pilot went over during the Dieppe raid and flew back and forth at 500 feet over the whole area, photographing the entire show. When he got back we counted no less than 125 holes in his Spitfire, all from ground machine gun fire.

Another time a Mossy came back after a cannon shell had exploded in the port engine. The pilot flew it home on one engine, and inside of four hours we had whipped the block off another kite and the Mossy was ready for action.

*   *   *

Thinking back, I still don't believe some of the things that happened in those wartime RCAF days. One time we were at Calgary – I think it was No. 3 Service Flying Training School – when a student pilot went off on a cross country flight. After a while, he decided he was out of gas, and so he landed in a farmer's field. Neither he nor the aircraft was hurt. Next, he was invited in for a magnificent home-cooked meal prepared by the farmer's wife and the proverbial farmer's daughter ....

Meanwhile, our crew was sitting around the hangar wondering where this clown could be. It looked like we were going to miss meal hour if he didn't hurry up. And we did miss it before we found out what had happened.

It seemed that the student pilot had gone merrily off to a barn dance with the farmer's daughter while we sat around waiting. Boy, were we hot when we found that out! But we were even hotter when we went to pick up the Cessna Crane and found over sixty gallons of gas in the "empty" tanks.

*   *   *

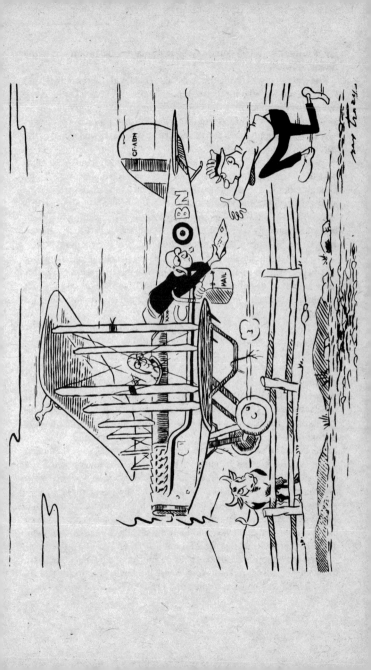

I was a fitter with 605 Auxiliary Squadron at Castle Bromwich in the middle thirties.

The squadron was flying the Avro 504, fitted with Lynx engines, and the Westland Wapiti with Bristol Jupiter engines. A general order came out calling for all training aircraft to be painted yellow, and our riggers set to work. When the first machine was finished – a nice job – it was taken out for photographs and positioned on the grass, well ahead of the apron and facing the airfield.

At the same time, a flying club pilot from the Midland Aero Club next door was making his first solo flight in a Gypsy Moth …. The photographer had set up his camera and tripod a little distance away for a side view of the 504. He had his head under the black cloth when this club pilot came in for a landing. And land he did, planting his Moth fairly and squarely on top of the 504, with his wheels through the top wing on either side of the centre section.

It was my best chuckle for a long time. I watched the photographer take his head from under the black cloth with an expression of amazement and sheer disbelief on his face. He surveyed the tableau in front of him and then bawled out, "Why the hell didn't you wait until I'd finished?"

All good clean fun and nobody hurt. But the club pilot didn't look very happy, sitting up there in the middle of it.

        *   *   *

We were flying Wimpy's out of Melsbroek airfield in Belgium and it was New Year's Day, 1945. New Year's Eve had been a night to remember for the festivities had been augmented by thoughts that the war would soon be over.

Things weren't so funny in the morning as we prepared to do a night flying test. Talk about hangovers! But big head or not we were getting the aircraft ready, when the Luftwaffe decided to wish us happy new year: ME 109's and FW 190's began strafing the airfield.

Now, Melsbroek had been camouflaged to resemble a farm when it was occupied by the Germans. Row upon row of cabbages had been planted between the runways and taxiways and there were a lot of these giant, overgrown cabbages still around.

When the bullets and cannon shells began lacing the field we all dove for whatever cover we could find. Some hid behind oil tins or battery carts. There was no time to pick and choose. When we were able to get our heads up to look about, we spied a Canadian pilot who stood over six feet tall. He was trying to shield himself behind one of the cabbages.

* * *

We were at Leicester in 1944, taking a conversion course prior to going out to 435 Transport Squadron in India. One night the weather was lousy: a lot of low cloud, smog, and crud. But we made it back to base around 0200 in the old Dakota. At least – we made it into the circuit. Somehow, we couldn't get permission to land from the control tower.

Well, that wasn't my problem. As the proud possessor of that most coveted of all aircrew flying badges, the estimable "O" Wing, I had managed to get us back home in spite of the weather. As the pilot and co-pilot now had things in hand, I started to clear out the maps and charts and make the area tidy, grateful that a couple of eggs and bed were just in the offing.

Wheels down, flaps down, steep descent ... wouldn't be long now. Suddenly, the two engines revved up, the aircraft took ascent position, flaps up, wheels up – and we climbed back to 1,000 feet. I walked up between the two drivers and asked, "What happened?"

"We got a red flare from the control tower just as we were about to touch down," the Captain said.

Round we went again in the circuit, threading between low driving scud, lining up for another approach. Wheels down, flaps down, steep angle of descent .... Another red Verey cartridge from the control tower!

The pilot was furious. He got on the blower and called the tower again. No joy. No response. Either the radio was U/S in the tower or unmanned or something.

Round we went again, same drill. And there was another red flare!

"The hell with it and to hell with those blokes!" the pilot said. "We're going in. This weather is going to get worse."

We landed, pulled off the runway at the first opportunity, and taxied to the dispersal area where we took a lorry to the mess.

Next day at lunch we were toasting our bums at the fireplace when an elderly British type, a pilot obviously of First World War vintage, started a conversation.

"Terrible weather, what?"

"Sure is," I replied. "I thought we were in trouble last night coming back from our navigational exercise about 0200."

123

"Oh! Were you that aircraft? I was in the tower and realized it was a bit dicey!"

"Yeah. Too much low cloud. I guess we were the last aircraft to come in."

"Yes! You were! Tried to help all I could, you know. Fired off Verey cartridges to help light up the runway."

*   *   *

One of our squadron's Lancasters ditched in the North Sea one night on its way back from a German target. It had been shot up pretty badly, and had lost two engines.

The crew did a commendable job of ditching in the darkness, and they all got safely into the dinghy and began paddling west towards England. The surprising thing was that the Lancaster refused, like the book said it should, to sink.

Another puzzlement was the dinghy itself, it seemed to be dragging anchor. Exploring for the reason the crew found that the water was only three feet deep, and that it contained a fine crop of seaweed. As dawn broke they could even make out what appeared to be a coastline, and they were mystified until the sun rose higher and they found themselves only 200 yards from shore. This revelation sent a cheer through the dinghy as they all climbed happily out and began wading ashore, pushing the dinghy ahead of them.

They came to an abrupt stop at the rattle of a machine gun. Then a stern voice told them to halt and not to move one inch. It was a navy shore patrol that had spotted them and found them merrily splashing their way through a minefield.

For You the War is Over

Until the publication of eye-witness reports of the horror camps at Belsen and similar places, perhaps no event so shocked the Allied world as the mass execution of the fifty air force officers who tried to escape from Stalag Luft III, in March 1944.

The cleverly contrived tunnel was a masterpiece of workmanship. The brains behind it were those of officers who had been planning escapes for some two or three years. They organized an escape committee (referred to as X for security reasons), under the leadership of a well-known RAF officer who was spoken of only as "Big X."

The project was a complex matter. The organization was split up into various departments: a tailor shop for the manufacture of civilian clothes; a carpenter and metal worker shop for making the tools to be used in the construction of the tunnel; a map making department; a compass making department; and a section for forging papers of various kinds. There was also an intelligence and security section.

Special prisoners who could speak German were designated "contact" men who would waylay the "ferrets" and invite them to their rooms for a cup of coffee in order to keep them out of the way and to bribe them to bring tools and other helpful accessories into the camp. No less important was the army of guards necessary to warn the various workers if any Germans were approaching. While work on the actual tunnel was in progress, every "ferret" in the camp was shadowed continually from the time he entered until the time he left. About one third of the whole of the North Compound had some share in the responsibility; but in spite of the numbers involved, there was never a leak to the Germans.

The tunnel entrance was very ingeniously concealed. It fooled the Germans completely, despite the several searches that were made. It was located in the last place in the world anyone would have expected to find it – beneath a stove. The stove stood on a tiled base which was supported, beneath the floor, by a four foot square brick wall, built below the raised hut. The square of tiles was removed from the floor and fitted into a tray which, when put back in position, formed an excellent trap door. It was so well done that even the cracks where it fitted into place were invisible.

Below the trap door, through the centre of the brick walls, a shaft was sunk straight down to a depth of thirty feet. This shaft, like the whole of the tunnel, was shored with wooden frames made from some 1,500 bed boards commandeered from every member of the camp. At the bottom of the shaft a special chamber was built for use of the labourers and carpenters.

The tunnel itself was over 350 feet long and about two feet square. Along the floor were wooden tracks on which a trolley ran, complete with flanged, tin-covered wheels, to convey the escapers. The track was built in three sections so that a person going from one end to the other would have to change twice on the way. The trolleys were rope operated by remote control. Ventilation was secured by means of a special air pump installed at the foot of the shaft, with a tin pipeline extending the length of the tunnel. Electric lighting also was provided, thanks to some light-fingered "kriegie" who stole a good length of wiring cable from the Germans.

The diggers had the hardest time of all. As the tell-tale dirt would have given the game away if they had worn clothes, they had to work either naked or in long underwear.

Another important consideration in the building of the tunnel was the dispersal of the sand. About fifty prisoners were put on dispersal squads. Each man made two long, thin, bags out of hand towels. These were tied to a long cord and hung down inside the legs of his trousers, the cord passing round his neck to take the strain. The bottoms of the bags were held together by a piece of string and a pin, which was attached to another piece of string leading to the pockets of the trousers. At the mouth of the tunnel, the bags were filled with sand while our guards kept watch. Then, the disperser wandered out to a sandy part of the camp where there was a volleyball or softball game in progress and, being careful that there were no German guards around, pulled the strings in his pockets. This released the sand, which he shuffled into the soil with his feet.

When time drew near for the opening of the tunnel, the names of all those who had worked on it were put into a hat. Out of some 500 people, 200 names were drawn. These would be the only ones allowed into the hut at the appointed time. On the morning of March 23, it was decided to break the tunnel that same night. The chosen 200 changed places with the regular occupants of the hut. Tense with anxiety they waited in the rooms till the time came for the opening.

At ten o'clock sharp, two expert tunnellers broke through the last few inches. To their dismay, they found that they were a few feet short of the woods in which they had intended to emerge, and only about seventy-five feet from a nearby Goon box. However, it was too late to change things. One volunteer stationed himself near the entrance to the tunnel to keep a lookout for guards and to give the others the okay to come through.

The order was then given to commence operations. Their pockets bulging with rations and escape kits, the prisoners hustled out one by one to make their fateful journey through the tunnel. They formed up in a small group in the woods to be conducted in a party away from the vicinity of the camp. The groups were formed at about half hourly intervals to give their predecessors a fair start in case any group should be caught.

The night could have been better, but it had its good points. It was snowing, which meant that tracks would be left, but there was also lessened visibility and a chance that the tracks could be covered. The wind was in a favourable direction, blowing down from the nearby Goon box, thus making noises less likely to be heard by the guard on duty. And there was, of course, no moon.

Then, while the night was still young, two unfortunate mishaps occurred. The first was a raid over Berlin, as a result of which all the lights were turned off and some time was taken in getting margarine lamps to serve as substitutes. The second delay occurred when someone became stuck in mid-tunnel and had to be rescued by his friends. These incidents considerably hampered the operations and more time was taken than had been foreseen.

At about five o'clock in the morning, just as dawn was breaking, a shot rang out. The game was up. One of the guards had seen a fugitive in the woods.

Immediately a hue and cry was raised. The commandant and an army of guards entered the camp. When they saw the array of prisoners completely packed and ready to leave, they could only surmise how many were already free. The commandant went stark raving mad. He ordered that all the people left in the hut be searched. Brandishing a revolver he threatened to shoot anyone who did not "jump to it." He had some reason to be worried as this meant a court martial for him. The members of each hut were then locked in until the Germans had made a photographic check of the entire camp. We learned that seventy-nine officers had escaped and our prayers went with them.

Four of the boys were caught immediately. They were brought straight back and put in the cooler. Rumour had it that some fifteen or twenty others had been rounded up, frost-bitten and completely exhausted. What had happened to the rest?

We learned on April 6, when we were assembled in the theatre for an address by the senior British officer. He walked on to the stage and addressed us as follows:

"Gentlemen, I have some tragic news to impart to you. The commandant has received a statement from the German High Command to the effect that forty-one of the officers who escaped have been killed." He paused to let the gravity of his words sink into our minds. Then he went on. "They state that these men were shot while attempting to resist arrest or to re-escape after being arrested. Obviously, this is the work of the Gestapo. A Luftwaffe officer told me personally that he deeply regretted the affair, and assured me that it had been taken out of his hands. In closing I ask you not to display a spiteful or vindictive attitude to the Germans. Let us show them we are men of discipline."

A few days later the following notice appeared on our bulletin board:

North Compound
Stalag Luft III
15 April, 1944.

The senior British officer regrets to announce the death of the following forty-seven officers who escaped on the 24th of March. The list of names was handed to him by the German authorities this evening.

P/O H. Birkland	F/O A.W. Kolanowski
F/L E.G. Bretell	F/L P.W. Langford
F/O L. Bull	P/O T.B. Leigh
S/L R.J. Bushell	F/L C.A.N. McGarr
F/L M.J. Casey	P/O G.E. McGill
S/L J. Catanach	F/O R. Marceskus
P/O A.G. Christensen	P/O H.J. Milford
P/O D.N. Cochran	F/O J.T. Mondechien
S/L L.K.P. Cross	F/O K. Pawluk
P/O H. Espelid	F/O H.A. Pickard
P/O B.H. Evans	F/O P.P. Pohe
P/O N. Fuglesang	F/O B. Scheidhauer
Lt. J.S. Gouws	P/O O.S. Skauziklas
P/O W.J. Grisman	Lt. A.J. Stevens
P/O A. Gunn	P/O R.C. Stewart
P/O A.H. Hake	F/O J.G. Stower
P/O C.P. Hall	F/O D.O. Street
F/L A.H. Hayter	F/L D. Swain
P/O E.S. Humphreys	P/O E. Valenta
P/O G.A. Kidder	F/O G.W. Walenn
F/O R.V. Kierath	F/O J.C. Wernham
F/L A. Kiewnarski	F/O G.W. Wiley
S/L T.G. Kirby-Green	S/L J.E.A. Williams
P/O J.F. Williams	

On May 19, a second notice announced:

> The senior British officer had notice this morning of the deaths of the following personnel:
>
> F/L J.L. Long
> F/O Z.S. Krol
> F/O P. Tobolski

This brought the total of those killed to fifty. Near the camp we built a vault wherein were sealed the cremated remains of twenty-nine of our dead comrades that had been sent back to us.

In spite of this German atrocity the mass escape was not a total failure. Three of the men got back to England, and eight of those who were recaptured were sent to concentration camps, from which they escaped again. The achievement of the former three in outwitting the Germans in the greatest prisoner hunt of the war shall always stand forth as a shining example of courage among the Allied nations.

*　　*　　*

In our POW camp, cooking was a full-time job, and anyone volunteering as cook got excused all other "stooge jobs."

One time, prompted either by culinary ambition or by the mistaken hope of a soft touch, a guy in our hut made us an offer. "I'll take over the cooking permanently," he said, "but only on one condition. No complaints. Just one complaint and I resign." Delighted with this unbelievable offer we all readily agreed to his proposal.

Everything ran smoothly for quite some time. But eventually the trials and tribulations of the kitchen began to show on the cook. He got tired of rushing back and forth to the communal camp stove with pots and pans. He got fed up with the scroungers always trying to cook out of turn or squeeze "just one small pan" on the stove. The endless struggle with the meagre food supply and the constant strain of finding new items for the menu finally wore him down.

He became more and more careless, burning the cakes, dishing up watery porridge, serving cold meals – anything to draw a complaint from us and so end his bargain. But we all maintained a stoic attitude, suffering each awful dish rather than complain and lose a cook.

In desperation, the cook made a pan of salty porridge that was burned to a dirty brown colour. We all stared at it in dismay, but preserved

our silence. The first man to taste the porridge grimaced horribly and looked at the cook. The cook glared back, silently, daring him to utter a word, just one word against the porridge.

"I don't feel hungry tonight," the man said. "I think I'll skip the porridge."

The second guy took a spoonful and swallowed it without thinking. He clutched his stomach and uttered a frightful howl.

"Where in hell did you get this crap?" he cried. Then, suddenly remembering, added quickly, "But it's damn well cooked!"

*　　*　　*

In March of 1945 I was one of many thousand POW's crowded into a compound at Lukenwalde, thirty-five miles southwest of Berlin. Lukenwalde was ill-equipped to house the vast numbers gathered there following the exodus from POW camps in the east. In fact, there were about 1,500 American GI's living under canvas.

Most important, food was practically non-existent. The daily ration was a half litre of watery soup and one slice of black bread per man. Nevertheless, spirits were exceedingly high. The American armies were less than forty miles to the west. Low flying Soviet aircraft were in the air daily, and RAF Mosquitoes were hitting Berlin with clock-like precision each night.

The popular guessing game was: "Who'll arrive first, the Yanks or the Russians?"

Then one misty morning in April the question was answered. At the break of day, tanks of the forward elements of the Soviet Army rolled ponderously through the camp, crushing, with gargantuan might, the hated barbed wire. The Germans, commandant and all, had left during the night.

The initial joy at being "free" soon faded, since the Russians showed a total lack of interest in our repatriation. Everything was in a state of flux until the Americans arrived to take us west. While we waited we did certain daily tasks. Seven of us volunteered to guard a former stores depot. Sporadic fighting was still going on around us as the Russians mopped up the last German pockets of resistance.

We were living in the largest of the three warehouse buildings, one that was stocked with all kinds of hardware. One night when we were asleep we were jolted from bed by a thundering crash. Then silence.

Suspecting Germans we grabbed the rifles we had acquired and snapped on the lights.

There was a lone GI, both arms wrapped tightly around a fifty kilo keg of nails, struggling to lift it off the floor. Around him was a shambles of small hardware items he had knocked off their shelves when he stumbled in. The sudden blaze of light scared the hell out of him. "Who are you?" he yelled.

The seven of us converged on him, and he began to explain his presence in tumbling words. "I didn't know anyone lived here – the door wasn't locked – I just came in and lit a match and here was all this stuff!"

"But *nails*?" we asked. "What the hell good are nails to someone living in a tent?"

* * *

We were flown to England, after getting out of the bag, by the RAF. They had Lancs and Hallies all over the place, flying back the thousands of Allied prisoners.

While I was standing on the tarmac waiting to board a Lancaster the young pilot asked me if I'd like to ride in the mid-upper turret. "We'll be flying over Vimy Ridge and you can get a splendid look at the Memorial," he said.

In our group there were a number of British naval personnel who were also POW's, and among them was an Admiral. Just before we took off, the rear gunner told the Admiral he could ride in his turret if he wished. The gunner himself would ride inside the fuselage.

About five minutes after takeoff the rear gunner decided he'd tell the pilot that he wasn't in his turret. "Skipper!" he shouted. "I've got an admiral stuck in my turret."

The pilot instantly put the aircraft into a violent manoeuvre, scaring the hell out of everyone. He thought the gunner had said: "I've got the aerial stuck in my turret."

Meanwhile, the Admiral was getting the ride of his life and he was yelling, "Is everything okay, skipper?"

One hour and fifty-five minutes after takeoff we landed in London. We were lined up and marched into a hangar where we were told to disrobe and stand naked. That was where they deloused us for the last time.

* * *

136

I spent VE Day in Brussels. Our POW camp had been liberated by the Russian Army, and after a month's wandering we had been flown to Brussels by the United States Air Force. The city was in a frenzy as everyone fought to get into the centre of the city to celebrate. There was no accommodation, the authorities said, and they tried to put us in a former prison. After spending years locked up in a German prison camp there was almost a riot. Those who didn't want to stay in the former prison could have 800 francs and seek their own place to sleep.

My friend Peter and I grabbed the francs and started off for the centre of town. We had to walk since every tram car was piled high with Belgians swinging from the windows and sitting on the roofs.

Walking down a side street we came upon a small shop, and decided to find out what 800 francs could buy: we had no idea if it would be worth eighty cents or eighty dollars. The store was a Mom and Pop operation with living quarters in the rear. The old fellow who served us took one look at our uniforms and the fistful of francs we were waving and the two apples we had picked up – and burst into tears.

We stood there in some dismay, wondering what we had done to offend him. Soon his daughter, a pretty young girl, came out from the back. She explained to us in perfect English. "You must forgive my father. He knew at once you were prisoners of war and he was overwhelmed with tears to think that you would offer to pay for two apples.

"When the Germans were here," she continued, "the SS would come every week. They'd go behind the counter and take whatever was in the till. If it wasn't enough, they would slap and beat my father.

"I think that the end of the war, and the fact that you were the first uniformed Allied men to come into the store, and your willingness to pay for a little thing like an apple just upset him emotionally. Please, just let my father have his moment of happiness. Take whatever you wish – we can ask no money."

Since it appeared that she was about to cry as well, we thanked her and left the store. The apples, the first we had tasted in several years, tasted like no other apple we ever had … or ever will have.

Fall Out the Officers

There was a graffito pencilled on the wall of a cubicle in the gentlemen's at an RCAF station. It said: "If the Commanding Officer calls, tell him I can only handle one shit at a time."

*   *   *

I had the pleasure of going overseas on the *Aquitania*, a quaint old tub that carried many thousands of Canadians to war. As a sprog Pilot Officer I shared a cabin with three Australian gentlemen who were also navigators and also Pilot Officers.

We were deep into our bunks, "pressing blankets" as the expression goes, when the horn sounded for boat drill one afternoon. We all thought the same thing – to hell with it.

Ten minutes later our cabin door flew open, and a loud, authoritative voice hollered, "Get up on deck!"

Without opening his eyes, one of the Aussies said, "Fuck off."

"What did you say, young man?" queried the authoritative voice.

The Aussie opened his eyes, and saw the large figure of the CO Troops, who happened to be a Group Captain, glaring directly at him. Leaping from his bunk, he ran to the Group Captain, placed his sleeve next to the Groupie's, and started counting the stripes.

On his own sleeve he counted: "One." On the Groupie's sleeve he slowly counted: "One, two, three, four. Jesus!" he cried, and scampered out the door.

The Old Man stood there flabbergasted for a moment, but suddenly, as the rest of us held our breath, he broke out into loud laughter. Then, his eyes twinkling, he said, "Better get on deck, boys."

*   *   *

Jimmy was from New Zealand and a "dinkum cobber" to use the NewZie colloquialism for good friend. In the spring of 1943 we were flying with the RAF's No. 35 squadron of Bomber Command. Before the year was out we were sharing a tiny room in a German POW camp.

The incident I recall most about Jimmy has nothing to do with flying or the POW camp. It centres around what I always considered a rather archaic military custom: saluting.

Jim and I, both aircrew Sergeants at the time, were in Cambridge when we walked past a young British Army Lieutenant. I saluted him, but to my surprise, Jim just nodded his head politely and said something about it being a nice day.

The Lieutenant swung around and came after us. "Sergeant," he barked at Jim, "you failed to salute me."

"You are absolutely right, sir."

"Don't you recognize the rank I hold, Sergeant?"

"You're a First Lieutenant in some kind of army outfit, I think," replied Jim.

The Lieutenant choked on his words. "I'm bloody well a commissioned officer of the Royal Engineers, Sergeant," he snapped. "And you failed to salute me!"

"Well, sir, it's just a misunderstanding on your part. We New Zealanders only salute officers of the Royal New Zealand Air Force. There is, however, one exception," Jim added gratuitously. "We *do* salute officers of the RAF, a sister service."

"That's a crock of horseshit, Sergeant! You know as well as I do that King's Orders and Regulations apply to all junior ranks in the matter of their paying respects by saluting." It seemed to me that the Lieutenant was becoming a bit unglued.

Jim just gave that innocent grin of his. "The regulation you claim as nonsense, sir, is straight out of your own KR, and if I may say so it is there for a very good reason."

"And what might that be, my opinionated young man?"

"You see," continued Jim, "New Zealand is a very small country. Quite isolated. Just two small islands tucked in between the Pacific and the Tasman Sea."

"I know all about New Zealand. We are talking about saluting!"

"Yes, sir, I'm just trying to explain why our regulations might differ in some degree from those of other Commonwealth nations."

"I'm listening," was all the Lieutenant said this time. I gather he was tiring.

"Well," Jim went on, "we are present in Britain at a time when the country is host to a multitude of nations. Army, navy, and air force personnel are here in a variety of uniforms. There are all shades and all colours – some rather bizarre, I might say, from a conservative viewpoint …." Suddenly, Jim beamed. "Sir, by confining our respects to those officers of our own forces we avoid the embarrassment of saluting in error. Who, for example, was that who just passed us?"

We all turned in the direction of the Guildhall. There, a rather handsome man was just about to enter. He was wearing a long blue coat with a scarlet collar bordered by gold piping. It had a half-belt in the back with four brass buttons on it. To complement this unusual "uniform" he wore a top hat.

"What do you think he is, sir?" Jim asked innocently.

"Damned if I know," snapped the Lieutenant angrily. And he hurried away across Market Square.

* * *

Shortly after my return to overseas duty, this time as a Squadron Leader, I was walking up Bath Road in Bournemouth. Ahead of me I spotted some hectic activity as an aircrew Sergeant Pilot busily flung salutes to a Pilot Officer who was standing in front of him.

When I reached them, the Pilot Officer snapped off a salute to me. I inquired what was amiss.

"Well, sir," explained the Pilot Officer, "this Sergeant passed me without saluting. I have ordered him to salute me 100 times."

"Fine," said I. "And how many times has he saluted so far?"

"Fifteen, sir."

"Well, then, I guess you had better carry on," I remarked. "But you surely have been taught that you must return every salute – plus the fifteen you already owe."

I walked away, leaving behind a very humbled Pilot Officer and an amused and thankful Sergeant.

* * *

We had a Station Commander who just loved parades. This guy was a Group Captain, and each week he could hardly wait for the full station parade which included about 1,000 men and women. To ensure that his voice would carry to the farthest corner of the rear echelon and not be drowned out by the band, he had microphones strategically placed to amplify his commands.

One day, with the massed parade standing at stiff attention awaiting the official inspection, the Group Captain let go with a rip-roaring fart. It was immediately broadcast all over the parade square.

In the stunned silence that followed, the Station Warrant Officer, who was one of the characters of the air force, yelled out: "Speak again, oh lips that have never known a lover's kiss!"

Whereupon the entire parade collapsed in laughter.

* * *

143

At one time during the war, at a flying training station, we had an unusually active Commanding Officer. He was always dreaming up ways to improve our efficiency, to speed things up and thus turn out more pilots. Not so his staff: we were convinced we were *already* doing twice as much as we should, and deeply resented the constant harping and prodding.

At one weekly staff meeting the CO gave his usual tirade about sloppy work, sloppy dress, sloppy deportment, and things in general moving at a snail's pace. We all had to realize that there was a war on, and we couldn't take all day on simple tasks. "We're going to speed things up on this base," he thundered. "Everything must be done faster and more efficiently. Speed things up and cut down on wasted time!"

Seated beside me was the station dentist, a Lieutenant from the Canadian Army Dental Corps. He sat there seething, for he was the only dentist on base and he already had enough work for a staff of three.

It was only a few days later that the CO had an appointment with this dentist to have a tooth filled. Our army friend drilled out a large hole in the CO's tooth, put his drill away, and said, "That's all for this time. See the nurse for your next appointment."

"What?" roared the CO. "Aren't you going to fill my tooth?"

"No, sir. Your time is up. Only ten minutes per patient. You'll have to make another appointment."

*   *   *

When we were stationed at RCAF Station Lachine, someone bought a bird and a fancy cage-and-stand and put it next to the bar in the officers' mess. It caused a great deal of curiosity from the bar crowd when it first arrived, but people soon got used to it and didn't pay much attention.

One night the CO walked in. He hadn't been in the mess since the bird arrived. He took a long look at it and asked, "What kind of a bird is that?"

"It's a cockatoo, sir," someone answered.

"Oh," said the CO. He paused for a moment and then remarked, "What we need around here is a cunt or two."

*   *   *

Our Air Officer Commanding was a very taciturn individual. He just didn't have any small talk. He spoke seldom and laughed less. But

"Now your first duty, Sergeant, will be to set up an Officers Mess!"

underneath the gruff exterior he was a very warm-hearted and sincere officer. However, to the uninitiated he was a fierce looking tyrant whom they went out of their way to avoid.

Each morning the Air Commodore was picked up by a staff car and driven to his office. One day, when his regular driver was ill, a new and nervous driver arrived to do the transporting. He appeared right on the dot. Getting out, he stood by the rear door, and when the Air Commodore came in sight he snapped off a real military salute. Once the car was underway he thought he would venture some small talk.

"It's a lovely day, sir," he began.

"When did you become a meteorologist?" barked the Air Commodore.

The word got around that the Air Commodore didn't have a sense of humour. It was said that he never laughed or seemed pleased about anything. Those who believed he couldn't laugh should have been in the mess the night his wife spied the newly arrived budgie bird.

The bird had been a member of the mess for only a week or so, but the boys at the bar had been successful in improving its vocabulary, mainly through endless repetitions of four-letter words. The Air Commodore's wife rushed over to it, and began a long speech in baby talk. Cooing and clucking, she kept telling the bird how pretty it was. The Air Commodore stood with the rest of us, silently watching this performance.

"Oh, aren't you pretty," his wife said, purring into the cage. "Tell me your name, pretty bird."

In a moment of silence, the bird finally spoke. "Bullshit," it said.

The Air Commodore let out one joyous bellow of mirth and went reeling into the bar. His laughter echoed through the mess as everyone joined in.

* * *

In Canada, Victory Bonds were urged upon everyone, young or old, including guys and gals in uniform. In wartime Britain, bond drives or rallies were also big and constant things. Often pieces of military hardware were used to focus attention on the cost of military equipment. A Spitfire would be parked in Piccadilly Circus as the focal point for a giant rally. It would be decorated with signs announcing that it cost $100,000 to build one. Entertainers and personalities gave freely of their time, bands and singers performed, and a leading light would give the message: "Buy Bonds."

Factories held these rallies at lunch time. Radio stations hammered away on the theme: "Give for Victory." Newspapers ran huge government ads and wrote thundering editorials on the wisdom of buying bonds. Posters were hung all over the major cities and millions upon millions of dollars were raised to support the war effort.

In the larger cities and towns of Britain you could hardly not know what was expected of you. But in the smaller villages and hamlets the incessant cry to support the war effort was less strident and more muted - as befits the pastoral settings of the country.

Near our base at Linton-on-Ouse was a tiny village called Newton-on-Ouse, and there, one beautiful summer Saturday, Rally Day arrived. The organizer was the acknowledged leader of the community. She owned a large and stately mansion set in a few hundred acres of farmland, and she had donated it to the government for the duration of the war. It housed Canadian aircrew.

This woman had asked the CO of our base to be the guest speaker for the bond drive, and he had accepted. On Saturday our Lady was everywhere at once in the tiny village (which really wasn't much more than a duck pond with a row of little grey houses around it). Clapping her hands and carolling, "Everybody out, everybody out – we must make a good showing," she did her best to gain the maximum crowd. She had chosen for her theme the slogan: "Do It Now." A handful of people stood around the pond on one side of which a farm wagon with some chairs had been placed. When the crowd was one deep around the duck pond, an RCAF staff car arrived with pennant flying and out stepped the Group Captain with two staff officers.

They all climbed up on the wagon and the Lady introduced the CO to the villagers, who stood as though nailed to the ground.

Beginning his speech, the Groupie said what an honour it was to be able to address the citizens of Newton-on-Ouse, and what a privilege it was to be able to contribute to the defence of Britain. "However," he said, "the important thing is to *do it now*."

This reminded the CO of the story of the bumblebee, who was gathering honey in a sunlit field of clover when he suddenly found himself in the dark, damp stomach of a cow. The bee was so mad he was about to sting the cow, but then he noticed some nearby clover. "I'll just gather the honey from this clover and then I'll fix that cow," the bee said. But after the clover he felt sleepy. "I'll just have a snooze and then I'll give that cow something to remember," he said. Instead of doing it right away he went to sleep. And when he woke up – the cow had gone.

The CO looked around expectantly at the good burghers. They all stared back. Utter silence. They were waiting for the rest of the story.

Finally, looking rather blank, the Lady got up and thanked the CO for his address, which she knew would bring support from the people of Newton-on-Ouse. After which the official party got into their car and drove off.

*   *   *

I was the Senior Warrant Officer on the base. One evening I was enjoying myself in the sergeants' mess when a ruckus broke out in the airmen's lounge. I realized the service police would take care of things, but something nagged at me to go and supervise the scene.

When I arrived the service police hadn't yet appeared, so I found the obnoxious character and placed him under close arrest. This action called for escorts to take him to the guard house and I yelled for two volunteers to do the escorting duties – you and you! Off they went with the prisoner between them.

When I had settled things down in the lounge and briefed the service police (who had finally shown up), I proceeded to the guard house to make the mandatory report in writing. But I arrived at the guard house to find the cells empty. No one knew anything about a prisoner under close arrest.

The two escorts I had chosen had obviously been buddies of the prisoner. It ruined my evening.

*   *   *

We sailed out of New York aboard RMS *Queen Elizabeth*, the world's largest ship, on June 1, 1944. She was crammed full with a complete American army division and a considerable number of RCAF types, not to mention a bevy of nurses.

Fantastic June weather prevailed, and it continued hot for the whole voyage; very conducive to torrid love sessions. I learned to avert my eyes when I viewed the milling throng of US troops on the main deck forward. Some of the sights lent themselves to dark suspicions about the sexual ambivalence of people too long at sea. But then, those nurses!

As a Troop Deck Officer I began to get paranoid. All I could talk about were the pairs of shoes I saw sticking out from under RMS blankets as I did my appointed rounds on deck. Oh, well, I consoled myself. As long as both pairs of shoes point upwards there could be no problem.

F/L CATHCART   F/O TAILWHEEL   F/L GASKET
    F/L SCALPEL   F/O CONKOUT   W.O. SHINYPANTS

Then one day – there they were! One pair of shoes pointed up, one pair pointed down, and both pairs were obviously being worn by males. This was too much, and I stripped off the blanket with a loud yell.

I had been set up. All the junior officers had realized my obsession and two of them set the trap for me. It was great fun for all, if, at the moment, slightly embarrassing for me.

But it was more embarrassing for the two pranksters who, just a week later at Bournemouth, were paraded in front of the CO of the Training Wing for being AWOL.

I was the CO.

*   *   *

We were in France in the early days of the war, flying Lysanders on Army Co-operation duties. My pilot was a sprog Pilot Officer with little regard for rules or regulations. Ours was a grass airfield, which suited my pilot since he was never fussy about taking off into the wind. Any old direction was good enough for him, as long as it was convenient.

One day, I was already settled into the hind end of the plane and the pilot had the engine running when the Flight Commander hollered at us from the ground. "Do you know the wind direction?" he shouted.

My intrepid pilot looked quizzical for a moment. Then he wet his finger, held it in the slipstream, and indicated that he was already into wind.

The Flight Commander was so furious that he jumped on his hat, shrieked a few oaths, and waved us away.

*   *   *

We were flying Harvards, the mighty Yellow Perils of the RCAF out of Uplands, just south of Ottawa.

A number of instructors were jaw-boning one day in the flight room when the observation was made that the wheels of an aircraft are stationary on touch down. What if, some genius declared, the wheels could be made to spin? Think of the rubber that could be saved. Especially from the ravages of student drivers.

We were reflective for a few moments, thinking about the question. Suddenly one instructor, who had been staring moodily at his Coke bottle, leaped to his feet. "Coke caps! That's it. Coke caps," he cried.

"What in hell are you talking about?" we all asked.

"Coke caps. Simply cut them in half and make little air scoops out of them and then attach them to the rims of the wheels. When the gear is lowered the caps will catch the slipstream and rotate the wheels."

Eureka!

His enthusiasm spread, and soon fitters and riggers had a Harvard all fitted out with the Coke caps. Test day drew near. By this time, everyone had heard about our scheme, especially the brass. It was announced that such a serious test could only be carried out by the Squadron Commander and the Chief Flying Instructor.

The day came. The immaculate Harvard was rolled from the hangar, Coke caps sprouting from the wheel rims, all of them expertly welded and pointing in the right direction. The brass climbed aboard, and finally the plane took off.

Half the station was gathered on the tarmac for the historic occasion as the Harvard eventually swung into a wide circuit and prepared to land. It was a text book approach as befitted a Chief Flying Instructor – except for the fact the wheels were still up. Had they forgotten to lower the gear?

As the Harvard crossed the perimeter fence the wheels finally came down (although they weren't turning). Settling into a three point landing, the Harvard floated nicely above the runway. Then, as it touched down, the plane suddenly shot fifty feet straight up, as though a spike had been rammed into its posterior. Twice more this happened before the tail rose majestically and the Harvard did an outside loop. There she rested, wheels upwards, Coke caps shining in the late afternoon sun – and two grim-faced senior officers hanging from their shoulder harness.

We all converged on the aircraft, and with tongues firmly implanted in cheeks managed to free the unhappy pilots. The Chief Flying Instructor, rising to his full height, addressed us with a shriek. "It seems not enough research was carried out. *You dumb bastards!* The bloody kite shook like a whore in a fit!"

"What," someone asked timidly, "did you do, sir?"

"Applied the brakes, of course, and set the parking brake," barked the instructor.

"You did remember to release the brakes before landing, sir?" we asked.

There was dead silence as the crowd began melting away.

The Paper War

It seems everything in this world has a pecking order – but the chain of command in a military unit is often unique.

Wing Commander to Squadron Leader:
As you know, there'll be an eclipse of the sun tomorrow. That isn't an everyday occurrence. March out the Cadets to the parade ground at 0500 hours. Dress will be working dress. They'll be able to see the phenomenon, and I'll give the necessary explanations. If it rains, there won't be anything to see, anyway, and the students can remain in their barracks.

Squadron Leader to Flying Officer:
The Wing Commander has given orders for an eclipse of the sun at 0500 hours tomorrow, in working dress. He'll give the necessary explanations of this rare phenomenon in the barracks.

Flying Officer to Flight Sergeant:
At 0500 hours tomorrow morning the Wing Commander will eclipse the sun in working dress with the necessary explanations on the parade ground. If it rains, this rare phenomenon will take place in the barracks, which is not an everyday occurrence.

Flight Sergeant to Aircraftsman Second Class:
Very early tomorrow morning at 0500 hours the sun will eclipse the Wing Commander in the barracks, in working dress. If it rains, this rare phenomenon will take place on the parade ground.

* * *

The RCAF had a career evaluation system that struck terror in most people. The officers' form was called an R-211. All promotions were based on it in peacetime. It was filled out by your superior officer once a year – R-211 time. A long list of multiple choice questions were supposed to rate your initiative, loyalty, ability to get the job done, and so on. Once the score was added up, a percentage was reached. If the officer being assessed fell below a certain per cent he had to sign the form in the presence of his superior. This was bad news and didn't augur well for future promotions. At the bottom of the form was space for a brief narrative, where the superior officer could support the grades he had given.

One officer had really given a junior officer a very bad assessment. He ordered him to sign it, and was expecting a great argument. Usually, a junior would try to talk his way out of a really bad assessment – at least to get it above the line where he wouldn't have to sign.

In this case, when the hapless junior saw what his superior had written, he immediately grabbed a pen. "Oh, I'll be glad to sign that," he cried. "That's perfect!"

The startled assessor snatched up the form to see what he had written.

It read: "I have taught this man everything I know and he knows nothing."

* * *

The most amazing promotion story took place at RCAF Station St. Hubert, Quebec, sometime in the middle fifties. I think it even made *Time* magazine.

The hero of the story was a Leading Aircraftsman who had failed to get promoted year after year. So many years went by that he had given up the thought of ever reaching Corporal, and he took no interest in the general excitement on the station when a new promotion list was published. It was totally unexpected when his Sergeant came running up to him in the hangar, clapped him on the back, and cried, "Congratulations, you've been promoted to Corporal!"

The man was so shocked that his mouth flew open – and it stayed open. His jaws had locked, and he couldn't respond except with bulging eyes and frantically waving arms. At first the other groundcrew howled with laughter. Finally, sanity prevailed, and they called the station ambulance. It was decided to rush him into the Montreal General Hospital.

The patient got into the front seat with the driver, and with his mouth open and the lights flashing and the siren howling they roared away to Montreal. When the ambulance stopped at some intersections the pedestrians waiting to cross the street were attracted by the siren and crowded around to see who was in the ambulance. They got to stare at the RCAF's newest Corporal who, in turn, stared open-mouthed back at them.

According to the driver, the crowds were quite willing to believe that his patient was making the noise they could hear from the siren.

* * *

The road to rapid promotion in wartime was open to you if two things happened at the same time. You had to be fighting in a very active war zone – and you had to survive. In less than fifteen months, Sailor Malan went from Flight Lieutenant to Wing Commander. He destroyed thirty-two enemy aircraft in that time, and he was awarded four decorations: two Distinguished Service Orders and two Distinguished Flying Crosses.

* * *

We were stationed at Coal Harbour early in the war when word came from Air Command Headquarters that all Senior NCO's were to be issued with Sten guns. Canada was very nervous at that time about being invaded by the Japanese.

When we went down to get ours at the Supply Section, we were handed a neatly sealed cardboard carton. We took it back to our room, threw it in a corner, and immediately forgot about it. It was months later, during an idle moment, that we decided to find out what was inside.

The gun, we found, was not assembled. There was just a jumble of parts without instructions. After fiddling with the various bits and pieces, trying, without success, to make them fit, we threw the box back in the corner.

"What the hell!" we said, with a laugh. "There isn't any ammunition, anyway!"

* * *

There was once a stores in which a quantity of air force clothing was kept, pending emergencies. In the stores there were rats, and to keep down the rats there was a cat – for which a small subsistence allowance was drawn monthly.

Retrenchment, however, was the order of the day; and the officer in charge was instructed to demand item Q12/587: "Traps, rat, wire, iron, galvanized, springtype, Mark I" – one trap to every 100 units of clothing. A material specification with an elaborate illustration and description of the above trap appeared, and the cat was retired and struck off strength.

If there was to be one trap to every 100 units of clothing, 19.3 traps would be required. Accordingly, twenty traps were demanded. The demand came back with one trap disallowed, but by way of consolation it was stated that "fractions of a trap exceeding .5 would be considered as a whole trap." The officer in charge of the clothing stores pointed out

that the odd thirty-three units of clothing would now be at the mercy of the rats, but to no avail.

When the nineteen traps duly arrived, a return of kills was ordered to be submitted monthly. The return in question (designed by Organization and Management), was arranged in birdcage form, and was a masterpiece of its kind. At a glance it showed the amount of clothing in stores, the cubic measurement of each room, the number of traps on hand, and the number of rats caught each day. Mice were to be listed under "Remarks"; the percentage of rats caught to items of clothing, and of rats to traps, was to be marginally noted; and as it was feared that the officer in charge of the clothing stores might endeavour to take credit for mice as rats, the measurements of the caught animals were to be inserted. The officer in charge was authorized to demand a "suitable service measuring rod for the purpose."

Anxious to show the keen interest taken in the matter, the officer in charge at Group demanded "gauges, measuring cartridges, and a live shell." These would enable measurements to be taken to 1/1,000 of an inch. In reply, the Chief Inspector of Explosives pointed out that the gauges were fitted with gunmetal screws and were intended for measuring explosive articles only, "a condition presumably not applying to rats"; that their use with articles of a non-explosive character would therefore be "highly irregular if not dangerous"; and that the operation must in any case be carried out under magazine regulations – with felt slippers in an isolated building 400 yards from a road. "A plan of the locality was to be submitted."

An application that the term "live shell" might be extended to include live rats was rejected, and it was suggested that an ordinary two-foot rule would be sufficiently accurate for practical purposes. Accordingly, a two-foot rule was requested; but the demand elicited the reply that "these stores formed part of chests, tool, carpenters" which were only provided when carpenters' shops were authorized. A strong case was therefore made for the erection of a carpenters' shop, and form A9 was submitted. It was eventually approved at the cost of some hundreds of dollars.

Meanwhile, the officer in charge of the stores acknowledged receipt of the traps and requested instructions as to how they were to be set. The reply came "that the matter had been under consideration by the Directorate of Armament Engineering, and instructions would shortly be published."

The time came for the first monthly return. It showed several items of

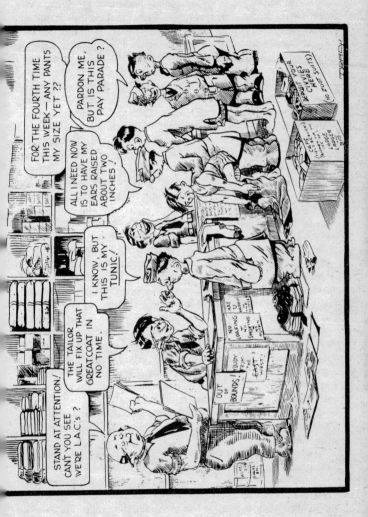

clothing destroyed by rats. The authorities thereupon gave evidence of the energy that they have always displayed in an emergency, and a very comprehensive pamphlet was issued by the Directorate of Training in which the mining of iron, the shaping of wire, the method of galvanizing, the manufacture of traps, and the system of trap inspection, testing, and acceptance were exhaustively discussed and profusely illustrated. Nevertheless, the second return was like the first.

"Were the instructions regarding the setting of traps strictly carried out?" came the query. "Yes; the clothing destroyed doubtless was part of that for which traps were disallowed," was the triumphant rejoinder. Another trap was therefore allowed but "it was intended to make a corresponding increase to the clothing stores of sixty-seven items of clothing." The third return showed "rats caught nil" and more clothing destroyed.

A Mark II trap was introduced which differed from the Mark I in that the iron was obtained in Germany. No rats were caught, and further destruction of clothing occurred.

"None but Group I tradesmen were to be permitted to handle the traps, and a Warrant Officer was to be struck off duty and detailed to instruct them. A return was to be submitted monthly showing the number of men instructed." In selecting the Warrant Officer, the claims of a man who had been a professional rat catcher were ignored, and the opportunity of infusing new blood into this important service was neglected. The grievance was duly aired in a weekly contemporary.

The worthy airman who *was* selected, elaborated a drill in accordance with "the spirit of instructions" which, after various extensionary motions to develop the trap-setting muscles, commenced with "take up traps" and ended with "ease springs." Badges in gold and worsted of crossed rats' tails were authorized for men who attained a certain degree of proficiency in trap setting. But still no rats were caught, and the destruction of clothing continued.

"The return showing the number of men instructed was to be submitted in duplicate once a week." Even this failed to produce an improvement.

And then it was suddenly discovered that the trap, though officially known as "Trap, rat, wire, iron, galvanized, springtype, Mark II" was in fact made of ungalvanized iron! The responsibility for this blunder could not be brought home to anyone, but after some discussion the nomenclature was changed and the material specification amended accordingly. This amendment was made retroactive, and past returns were ordered to be resubmitted. They were still found to be blank, however, and no improvement ensued.

The authorities were reluctantly compelled to admit "that the traps had not answered their expectations and that there appeared to be no fault either in the traps or the setting." They inquired, incidentally, what bait was used ....

This was when the officer in charge of the stores pointed out that no allowance was made for bait in Finance Regulations, and that he could not be expected to provide it out of his own pocket!

In the end, the cat was re-enlisted under provisions of air force regulation 458. It was to be used "strictly for the purpose of catching rats." The traps were ordered to be retained "for instructional purposes only," and an Establishment Table was raised.

VIP's

During a wartime visit to a heavy bomber squadron, King George VI and Queen Elizabeth were inspecting the aircraft and crews. The crews were standing to attention under the nose of their particular aircraft, and the King and Queen were introduced to each crew member as they proceeded down the line.

When introducing the captain of one crew, the CO mentioned that the pilot came from Brazil. This caused interested comment from the King, but it was the Queen who spied some Portuguese writing on the nose of the bomber. She asked what the words meant.

A long stumbling pause ensued as the pilot turned to stare at his aircraft's nose, as though he were seeing it for the first time. Finally he translated the words into something innocuous, and the Royal Party moved on. No one was ever sure if those literate people knew how "Get Stuffed" looked in Portuguese.

* * *

Every military person has suffered countless visits to their base of "personages." The troops know, all too well, the wholesale preparations demanded of them, down to the last miserable detail: the extra hours, the endless cleaning, the practice parades, the fly pasts, the painting, the mess receptions, the formal inspections. And then, of course, the personal polishing and pressing and getting of haircuts. All these tasks, and more besides, fill up weeks before the brief event.

"The Queen is coming," is enough to render a grizzled Sergeant Major permanently paralyzed and send the most senior CO into shock. Not to mention his wife. Of course, for Royal Visits the whole country enters a zombie-like state. Every conceivable event is proposed, debated, studied, conferred over, and enlarged beyond life itself.

As a public relations officer in the RCAF I suffered my share of visits – but with the advantage of being privy to some delightful not-on-the-agenda-details that made some visits livable and put lots of things into perspective. Personally, I found that Royal Visits made more sense and were more rewarding than all the others combined.

In the 1950s, "Bounce" Weir was perhaps the best float plane pilot in the RCAF. He was a natural choice for duty when a VIP had to be flown into a remote area of Canada. Accordingly, when His Royal Highness Prince Philip wanted to do some salmon fishing out of Goose Bay, it was Bounce who was chosen to fly an Otter float plane in from Ottawa. He was to fly the Duke into the RCAF fishing camp at Eagle River,

F/O DEADLINE   "THE PRESS"

about twenty miles northeast of the base. It had some of the best Atlantic salmon fishing anywhere in the world.

The press party which was covering the visit wasn't allowed to accompany the Duke to the fishing camp. As press escort I sat around with them at Goose Bay, helping them to destroy the mess. We all gathered at the wharf on the day of departure when Bounce and the Duke taxied out for takeoff. It was a beautifully smooth takeoff, and the knowledgeable people in attendance nodded and said: "You can always tell when Bounce takes one off."

Two days later, we all watched the landing on their return. It was letter perfect, the Otter sliding onto the glassy water with scarcely a ripple. "You can always tell," said our group in unison, "when Bounce puts one on."

When the Otter taxied in, there was Bounce grinning from the left hand seat. The Duke was in the right hand seat.

Later, at the bar, I cornered Bounce. I wanted some information on what had gone on in the camp. Some tidbit the press could hang a story on. But he was noncommittal. All I could extract was: "He's a great guy. We all had a great time. The fishing was great." Despite countless questions that's all I could get out of him.

Months later, for my own satisfaction, I tried again to find out how the two had gotten on. "Surely to God, Bounce, the Duke said something of interest?"

Bounce finally turned to me. Before he spoke he looked carefully around the room. "You won't say anything to anyone will you?"

"About what? Hell, it's too late now, anyway."

"Well, that wasn't me flying the Otter."

"You mean the Duke did the takeoff?"

"Yeah."

"For God's sake why didn't you tell us when it happened?"

"Didn't think it was my place to say anything. He did the landing, too."

I continued to dig. "Did he say anything? He must have thanked you!"

"When we were getting out of the aircraft he said, 'Bounce, if you're ever in London, look me up.'"

On another occasion in the 1950s, Prince Philip visited a small RCAF base in the Yukon. It caused the usual flurry of activity. Hardly equipped to handle a Royal Party, complete with massed entourage, the unit did what it could to provide some semblance of *décor*.

Short on kitchen and mess staff, the CO recruited some local ladies from a nearby village to help serve the meals. While they were enthusiastic workers, their idea of etiquette lay on the functional side.

One enterprising waitress was removing Prince Philip's plate when she cautioned him, "Keep your fork, Duke, there's pie coming." Perhaps such untoward incidents were welcome interludes from the more pompous and stultifying official functions most visiting dignitaries had to suffer.

On another Royal Visit, the Queen and Prince Philip arrived in Ottawa after attending the Queen's Plate in Toronto. The guard of honour was commanded by a young Sabre jet pilot, who had been instructed to chat with the Queen during the formal inspection. This, some genius had decided, would relax Her Majesty and so make the event less solemn.

The guard commander did as he was told. Halfway through the inspection, as they paraded down a file, he summoned up his nerve and addressed the Queen.

"I understand, your Majesty, that you were at the races yesterday."

"Oh, yes," replied the Queen. "It was the annual Queen's Plate."

"Did you make any money, ma'am?"

The Queen stopped dead in her tracks, trying with difficulty to hide her merriment, while the crowd of dignitaries stared in wonder.

And then there was the occasion when Queen Elizabeth was touring Canada, and she had to inspect a departure guard of honour in a rainstorm. She was quite distressed as she entered the C-5 aircraft and was met by the steward, Warrant Officer Jerry Mignault. "Oh, dear," said the Queen. "I'm afraid I've ruined these shoes."

"Ma'am," Jerry replied, "if you'll let me have them, I'll see what I can do." The Queen slipped off her shoes and handed them to Jerry before going to her compartment in the rear of the aircraft.

Taking the shoes to his galley, the Warrant Officer popped them into the radar range, the forerunner of today's microwave oven. In a few minutes, he was returning the completely dry and renovated shoes to a smiling and delighted Queen.

*　　*　　*

The spring of 1955 found me as CO of Frobisher Bay on Baffin Island. It was a hectic time, because I was also Co-ordinator Dew-line logistics.

One of the critical items in that corner of the world was the daily weather report. We invented a new term to more aptly describe flying conditions. While the official meteorologists continued to use the acronym CAVU (Ceiling Absolute Visibility Unlimited), we used the term CAFB when reporting our weather to Goose Bay.

Presumably, this *could* be interpreted as "Clear As a Fucking Bell" – although we protested that it meant "Clear At Frobisher Bay." Despite our protestations, the former term became more popularly used, especially by visiting aircrew.

It was during this time that Prince Philip made a visit to Goose Bay. He had been visiting the Western Arctic, and came through Goose Bay for some fishing prior to going home aboard the Royal Yacht *Britannia*, which had sailed into port for that purpose. While the Duke was off fishing we did our best to teach the *Britannia* crew how to handle Goose Bay liquor.

A large party was organized in Prince Philip's honour, and the guests included American personnel (and their wives) from the United States Air Force which occupied the other side of the base. Imagine my chagrin when, during the party, one of the leading American ladies asked me, quite innocently I believe, what I meant in my weather reports when I sent out the initials CAFB.

Since I was feeling no pain, I was able to reply with complete candour. Much to the Duke's amusement.

*   *   *

Royal visits weren't the only special events that could produce excitement in the RCAF.

When General Montgomery came to Canada ten years after the war, he paid a visit to Air Command Headquarters at Lachine, Quebec. I was instructed to provide photographic coverage. Montgomery couldn't have been more charming. As soon as he spied the camera he was all business, arranging every photo down to the last detail. He told what people to stand where and how they should turn their heads. We kept the camera flashing long after we had run out of film. I had the impression he would have happily posed all day.

Winston Churchill also visited Canada after the war. He was such an historic figure that he turned all our External Affairs people into jelly. They lost whatever common sense they had at the mere sight of him.

The night in which Churchill departed from Rockcliffe air base was a cold and wintry one. The farewell dinner at Government House had been long and merry, and the RCAF aircrew had delayed and delayed

171

the departure time. Our group of press people were standing around on the tarmac, bitching and waiting in the cold.

Finally, with a great bustle, the official motorcade arrived, escorted by countless RCMP types and excited External Affairs personnel. The Prime Minister and half of his Cabinet plus many members of Parliament jostled around at the foot of the ramp, all of them eager to be in the great man's company until the last possible minute.

Churchill was engulfed by the mob, and he hardly seemed to know where he was. Long minutes dragged by in the cold as farewells were said over and over again – and still Churchill made no move to board the aircraft. After a time it became obvious that he was too far gone to realize what was happening, where he was, or what he was expected to do. As we all stood crowded together in the dark, it seemed to our press party that the poor man would surely freeze to death. My moment in history had arrived. Stepping forward, I took his arm. "Sir, the aircraft is ready," I said, and led him to the foot of the ramp.

Churchill gave a small jump as though startled. Then his eyes cleared. "Quite right," he said. "Must be off."

With that, he began climbing the stairs. Halfway up he turned and gave his famous two-fingered victory salute. The crowd cheered as he wended his way into the aircraft.

*　　*　　*

And then there were the enjoyable days when Air Chief Marshal Trenchard visited Canada. Lord Trenchard, nicknamed "Boom" for his great voice, was considered the Father of the RAF. The RCAF would gladly have adopted him as their father. He sat in the cockpit wherever he travelled, and delighted the crews with his enthusiastic comments. Flying over the prairies he would boom out, "God, it's magnificent, just magnificent!"

I was delegated to record his arrival at Rockcliffe air base one sunny afternoon. He was arriving by RCAF Dakota aircraft, and was to be met by Air Marshal Frank Miller and Air Commodore Remington, the British Liaison Officer. My photographer and I were standing to the left of the short ramp, ready to record the event. The Air Marshal and Air Commodore were standing on the other side.

When Trenchard emerged from the aircraft, I was the first thing he saw. "Hello, there!" he boomed out, his voice carrying across the airfield. "My God, but it's good to see you again." He came down the three short steps, smiling and reaching out to shake hands with me.

I was so startled and so busy saluting and shaking hands that I couldn't find any words. But I was conscious of the glares I was getting from the official greeters. None of it fazed Trenchard, and he gave the Air Marshal the same boisterous greeting.

When Lord Alexander was Governor General of Canada in the immediate post-war years he was an inveterate traveller with the RCAF, flying to every nook and cranny of the country. He was one of the best-liked passengers we ever carried, and he loved to visit the most northerly regions and outposts. The absence of regal trappings in those remote areas never bothered that famous soldier. In fact, he seemed to enjoy the rough going.

One day, he landed for an overnight stop on South Hampton Island, where the RCAF had a tiny detachment. It was an occasion for celebration by all ranks, and the merriment continued right through the night, long after the official party had retired.

Alexander was an early riser, and when he awoke the next morning he decided to find the kitchen and something to eat. He didn't realize that the cooks hadn't been to bed. They and the kitchen were in great disarray when, clad in his pyjamas, he entered the room and politely inquired whether it was possible to get some breakfast. Too far gone to recognize him, the cooks responded with a loud shout: "Get your own fucking breakfast!"

It was the measure of the man that he considered the episode a great joke, and so the official wrath of the RCAF was denied.

Another of the well-liked VIP's to fly with the RCAF was Louis St. Laurent. When he was Prime Minister he and 412 squadron made their first round-the-world flight together.

The trip, however, was made without Mrs. St. Laurent, who refused to fly anywhere at anytime. When the C-5 aircraft departed Rockcliffe air base she would not even climb the steps to the aircraft – and it was the same when the flight returned. Her husband had to descend to solid earth before he got his homecoming kiss.

The crew remembered that trip because of the PM's constant consideration of their welfare, something that was quite often ignored by other VIP's. A few days before leaving Japan to fly home, for instance, he gathered them together and told them he didn't think they would have any difficulty with Customs when they arrived back in Ottawa.

As a result of that quiet tip, a couple of disbelieving but delighted wives got oriental rugs as their homecoming gifts.

*   *   *

When the Prime Minister of Australia visited Ottawa for the first time, the Canadian Broadcasting Corporation, (CBC), decided to do a live broadcast of his arrival. Ken Brown of the CBC was to be the commentator. Mr. Menzies arrived aboard the RCAF's C-5 aircraft – the pride of the fleet. A large press contingent was on hand that dark night, all of them eager to get some words of wisdom from the crusty, taciturn Aussie.

As the aircraft taxied to a stop, Brown was busy describing the scene over a live mike, his voice going over the nation's airwaves.

"Ladies and gentlemen, the Prime Minister of Australia has now stepped onto Canadian soil," he said, and then thrust his microphone into the PM's face. "Sir, do you have anything to say to the people of Canada?"

"No," Menzies barked, and immediately burrowed his way into the crowd, leaving Brown to recover his wits.

*   *   *

Over the years I took part in many tours of dignitaries from many nations but the one that impressed me the most happened at Baden-Solingen, Germany, home of No. 4 Wing of the RCAF's Air Division.

Prince Philip flew an RAF four-engined Heron aircraft into the base just a few days before Christmas. He was full of good humour, and talked to everyone he encountered, speaking in German to the civilian waitresses.

Over lunch that day he gave an impromptu talk. Without a note he made the best address I ever heard delivered to military personnel. I know exactly what he said – for I had hidden a microphone in a bowl of flowers on the headtable and recorded every word. I think the speech makes just as much sense today as it did back in 1963 when Prince Philip said:

We are inclined to forget, among all the chat about deterrents and alliances and freedom of the Western World, what all this means in human terms.

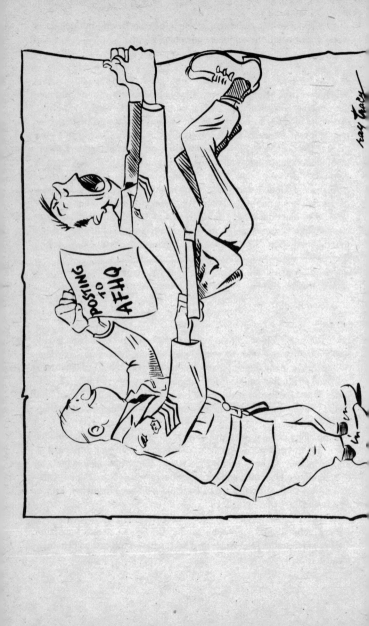

All of you here on this base in Germany, living far from home among strange customs and a strange language, represent the price that we have to pay in terms of people to maintain this alliance and to be ready for any eventuality. It may be easy enough on paper to move squadrons and divisions and ships and men around the world, but none of this movement would be the least bit effective without the willing co-operation of the people who are, in fact, pushed around. I would like to pay tribute to the willing co-operation of all Canadian servicemen and their families who are stationed in Europe.

You may not be the biggest contingent in the alliance – but you are a vital part of its strength and stability. After all, anybody can work up patriotic fervour in times of crisis and war, but it needs a very special kind of patience and determination to remain alert and prepared during the quiet periods and the lulls.

It is a favourite pastime among armchair strategists (who should know better), to tote up the numbers of ships and divisions and work out the relative strengths of various parties in international affairs. However, such exercises omit one very important and essential factor, and that is the quality of the people involved in these units. It's the morale and discipline and determination – the human factors – which are decisive in any assessment of the strength of any organization.

This human factor counts from the very top to the very bottom because it matters in the simple or not-so-simple business of the design of the equipment; it matters in the selection of the equipment; and it goes right-the-way through the composition and organization of the services and right through, finally, to the courage of one single man in the face of the enemy.

The whole object of this defence effort (and, after all, it takes a considerable taxation effort to maintain), is to protect our independence as individuals and nations and to ensure that we can continue to live our way of life as free and honest and upright people. The better this way of life – the more convinced we are of what we want – the more we will be prepared to sacrifice to defend it. Equally, the greater the price of our defence, the more convinced we should be to see that our way of life is, in fact, what we would like it to be. These two things hang together. You cannot be enthusiastic about a rotten and corrupt society and, however splendid a society, it cannot be defended by lazy and inefficient services.

In my personal knowledge of the Canadian services they are setting a very high standard indeed. And I am certain that this tradition will be maintained in the future.

Shatterproof and Prune

Warrant Officer Ray Tracy, a native of Fairville, New Brunswick, was known to many thousands of RCAF personnel through his work as a graphic artist and cartoonist. His deft illustration of service manuals and texts brought many a smile to the faces of studious trainees. His posters and drawings caught the eye, and reflected his keen observation and warm sense of humour.

Tracy joined the RCAF in the fall of 1940 as an aero-engine mechanic. It was not long, however, before his abilities as a draftsman and artist became known, and he was called upon to fill many demands at stations in Western Air Command. This was where he served most of the war years.

In 1945 his trade classification was changed, and he devoted full time to graphic arts. He was closely associated with the RCAF magazine, *The Roundel*, from its beginning in November 1948. His portrayal of Editor Rick Mignon's fictitious character, Sergeant Shatterproof, met with immediate approval, and the Tracy drawings continued for more than eight years to illustrate the popular series.

It was in Ottawa, shortly after a flying visit to Italy and Egypt, that Tracy died suddenly of a heart attack on May 12, 1958. He was thirty-seven years old.

*   *   *

Aircrew stationed in Britain during the war were entertained each month by the most famous pilot in the RAF: Pilot Officer Percy Prune. He was the aircrews' hero – always in the deep stuff, always on the carpet or being court martialed for pranging an aircraft. We all totally identified with this fictitious character, who graced the pages of a tiny flight safety publication called *Tee Emm* (an acronym for Training Memorandum).

It was, of course, the tremendous style of the writing and cartooning which made *Tee Emm* an unforgettable success with aircrews. There was not a hint of "officialdom" anywhere. No stern, stereotyped messages, no pontificating on various do's and don't's. Just the escapades of an innocuous-looking pilot – escapades that everyone could recall having come close to duplicating at one time or another. The difference was that Prune's were printed, and in such a refreshingly humorous manner that the rest of us absorbed the serious lessons while doubled over with laughter.

The man responsible for bringing Prune to life was W. "Bill" Hooper. He recalled that it all happened this way:

In the spring of 1941 I had just completed the cartoons for a book called *Forget-Me-Nots For Fighter Pilots*. It was written by my CO, Squadron Leader James "Prof" Leathart, from lessons learned on 54 squadron in the Battle of Britain.

It was at this time that I received an invitation from Flight Lieutenant Anthony Armstrong Willis to come up to the Air Ministry in order to discuss a possible cartoon figure that would permeate the pages of a lightly written, but utterly serious, training memorandum for aircrew. The outcome was a meeting in the Holborn Grill at the end of Kingsway, London. A meeting of just three: Anthony Armstrong, MC; Wing Commander Joe Stewart, DFC; and myself.

In an atmosphere of *bonhomie*, beer, and pipe smoke, a name for the training memorandum, *Tee Emm* was decided upon. I then sketched an egg-headed pilot officer on the white marble-topped bar of that Edwardian grill. I suggested that we call the fool by the same name that, at my school, we had called any clot – Prune. So Percy Prune was born.

Prune astounded even those who had served in the air force since the time (as he would say), when the Air Ministry was a tent, Pontius was a pilot, and the British were painted blue, not wearing it. He himself sometimes claimed long service: "When I was first in we didn't fly the Channel. At that time Britain was joined by a land bridge to the continent." By carefully spaced court martials which regularly deprived him of seniority, he managed to serve through the entire war as a pilot officer.

He quickly became a legend. The Aircrew Refresher School at Brighton, a limbo for unfortunates who had "bent" aircraft, was nicknamed "Prune's Purgatory." "Prunery" meaning any foolish mistake, became a common RAF word, as did the verb "to dedigitate" (to get the finger out). Prune's portrait as drawn by Bill Hooper was instantly recognized wherever the air force operated.

Prune's cavalier attitude towards flying made him the perfect Horrible Example for the edification of aircrew. His dictum "Landing with the undercart up is just a mistake," was quoted in self-defence by many a student pilot. Low flying was one of his specialties, as witness these gems culled from his testimony before various Boards of Inquiry: "I prefer the Rotol propeller to the D.H. – the blades are three inches shorter, allowing me to fly lower .... " "I never pull the stick back when flying low in case my tail wheel hits the ground .... " "I was flying along the main road in a Maggie against a strong head wind – when an Austin 7 hooted and overtook me." No wonder that Flying Officer Fixe, his harried navigator, used to complain that Prune flew so close to the deck over the Channel that he had to stand up to see over the waves – or that the pitot tube, taking in spray instead of air, was registering fathoms per second instead of indicating air speed.

But Prune bumbled blithely on, "flapless while others flap," emerging unscathed from an horrendous series of catastrophes, his wake littered with crashed planes. His war record was described as "distinguished – or rather notable." His score of "destroyed or damaged" ranged all the way from Maggies to Manchesters, from Ansons to Spitfires. However "bent" the aircraft, Prune always emerged bloody but unbowed. Perhaps the lucky horseshoe which he carried in his pocket (despite its adverse effect on his compass), was the explanation.

Prune was equal to any task. He could fly anything, nearly. Even a temporary grounding in an administrative job didn't bother him a bit. He rapidly reorganized the staff to such an extent that the Air Officer Commanding agreed that Prune might well be returned to flying duties. His desk held nine baskets: In (full), Out (empty), Back Again, Action, For Attention, Forgive, Forget, Avoid, and Salvage.

On return to an operational squadron ("No need to remember things here, the way you had to at HQ"), he could be found at the bar making these comments: "My flying is so good the Direction Finding Stations get fixes on me to find out where they are .... " "It's not really flying blind: the instruments aren't in Braille .... " "My landings are so good I have to call up Control to find out if I'm on the deck .... " "I bounced so high when I first touched down that I had to slip off height to get in." To other pilots who frowned on Prune's actions, our doughty hero would reply, witheringly: "I've spent more time rolling off the top of loops than you have flying straight and level; so pipe down."

When others committed "pruneries," Pilot Officer Prune selflessly shared his glory with them. The Most Highly Derogatory Order of the Irremovable Finger was founded. Prune immediately, deservedly, became its distinguished patron. Every month one or more awards of this Order were announced. Some of the citations were very interesting:

To a Flying Instructor, for showing his pupil what to avoid: "After beacon flying at night, the instructor landed unwittingly at the wrong aerodrome. He then got out and sent the pupil solo. The pupil landed at base."

To a Pilot Officer, for the best and quickest reply to an inquiring instructor: "When asked by his instructor what action he would take if, when approaching to land, he heard the undercarriage warning horn, he replied: 'I should open the throttles slightly to stop the horn blowing and upon landing would remove the fuse.'"

To a Group Captain, for supremely quick recognition: "A navigator on his station was taking shots with his sextant when the Station Commander motored past. Seeing the navigator he at once stopped his car, reversed, and bawled out, 'Who gave you permission to use a camera?'"

To a Flight Sergeant Instructor, for exceptional quick-witted resourcefulness: "On telling a pupil to go and practise instrument flying he was informed by the pupil that his aircraft had no hood. To which the instructor replied: 'Well, then, close your eyes or something!'"

To a Group Captain, for navigation, repeat, navigation: "On arrival at a station, flying a Tiger Moth, he was very guarded in his remarks to the Duty Officer and others, merely asking his way to the mess. On arrival at the mess he was still remarkably silent until, on some pretext, he managed to get a glimpse of the Daily Routine Orders. He then became quite fluent and conversational – having at last discovered at what station he had put down."

The award (sometimes with extra citations for Marked Devotion to Asininity, Thinking One Cockpit Button as Good as Another, Touching Faith in the Ability to Estimate Altitude by Eye, or Overwhelming Tenacity of Purpose in the Face of Logic), became famous throughout the Commonwealth air forces. The pilot who burned his aircraft on crashlanding in France, only to discover that his confused navigation had in reality brought him to a ploughed field a couple of miles from the nearest English pub, was one winner. Another was the lad who couldn't understand how he hit the control tower (forty feet high) when his altimeter was definitely registering 100 feet.

Air force types will never forget staring in awe as the scruffy figure with the top button of his tunic missing (it had been shot off in a dog fight), wandered across the tarmac at RAF Station New Heary (Group Captain Max Boost, commanding), his faithful wire-haired terrier Binder scampering at his heels, forever attentive to his master's vice.

*   *   *

*P.O. Prune's definition of a good landing
is one you can   walk away from.*

Air Commodore N.R. "Nellie" Timmerman, who was the first Canadian to command an RCAF bomber squadron during the war (No. 408 squadron), tells of the time he met A.A. Willis, the creator of Pilot Officer Prune:

I had the pleasure of meeting the creator of Pilot Officer Percy Prune in June, 1941, when he visited our squadron at Scampton, Lincolnshire. We were engaged at that time in the normal bombing effort on Germany, but because we were equipped with Handley Page Hampdens, had the additional task of laying mines at low level in all the ports and harbours of Europe from France to the Baltic, a singularly unrewarding and highly dangerous operation – for the aircrew at least. The Admiralty, however, thought that we were doing just fine.

This mine laying operation was called "Gardening," and each minefield to be laid and tended from time to time was named after a vegetable, a flower, or a fruit. There must have been exceptions to this, for a check in my log book reveals that "Jellyfish" was the code name for Brest Harbour when the pocket battleships *Scharnhorst* and *Geneisenau* were there – but this was probably an intelligent anticipation of the state of the aircrew before, during, and after this operation.

At debriefing, a Personal Experience Report was written by each aircraft captain, explaining how things had gone. Pilot Officer Prune's creator was so intrigued by all this that during his visit he produced the following literary gem which I have treasured ever since.

PERSONAL EXPERIENCE REPORT

Crew:	P/O Prune		Date 22/6/41.
	Sgt. Straddle		
	Sgt. Shootaline	83 Squadron	M.S.I. No.
	Sgt. Duffgen		

Task: Shooting up Air Ministry, Gardening Raspberries.

Time out:	Time over target:	Time in:
21.00.	21.40	22.10

Any signals or procedure difficulties:
Twice accosted in Leicester Square.

Any other difficulties:	Task successful or not:
Refusing.	Successful.

Route out was via Piccadilly Circus Bar, Regent Palace Bar, Leicester Square (where we nearly lost Sgt. Straddle, by night interception), Criterion Bar, and all the Bars to the East. A large amount of light blonde flak was met in the Strand, but avoiding action was successfully taken. On arrival at the target there was considerable haze due to doors of several civil servants' offices being left open. Luckily the main doorway was visible through a clear patch and we made a trial run for it, the rear gunner having a brief encounter with a hostile taxi driver who had to pull up short, firing several bursts of incendiary language. At the doorway both heavy and light bumph was thrown up at us, but we took avoiding action, jumping into a side door further down. A pin point was obtained on the Air Council Room, several more were left on the Air Council Chairs, and finally the Vegetable (a raspberry) was left on the Air Council Table for them to view with Displeasure next morning. The run back was without incident up to Piccadilly Circus. Here Sgt. Duffgen was jettisoned. He landed early this morning, his excuse being that he had been kept by a delayed action blonde.

Signed:

P. Prune, P/O

* * *

We were stationed at Market Drayton flying Spitfires. One of our pilots was an American, Flying Officer Bill Conway. He was the most cheerful type you could meet, and totally extroverted. He kept things moving at all times and thoroughly enjoyed the English surroundings.

One night, on his way home from the pub, he was stopped by a Constable who gave him a ticket for not having a lamp on his bicycle. When the Bobbie asked his name, Conway replied, "Pilot Officer Prune."

The following day the loudspeaker broadcast a call for Pilot Officer Prune to report to the Adjutant's office. Conway decided he'd go along with the gag he had started, and duly reported. At the office, a Constable gave him a summons to appear in court on the following Wednesday.

In court, when they called for Pilot Officer Prune, the Judge began to laugh. The charge was read and Conway pleaded guilty. The Judge fined him "ten bob."

Conway yelled out: "Time to pay, your Honour?" To which the Judge replied: "A fortnight."

Conway came triumphantly back to base to report that it had been just a great time, that the court had been most cheerful, and that everyone had treated him fine. He thought his experience was well worth $2.22.

* * *

Any groundcrew type charged with the responsibility for maintaining some part of an aircraft knew about Gremlins. A lot of aircrew also

188

discovered them when, for some inexplicable reason never to be known, the aircraft would malfunction. The radio that gave only static; the machine gun that wouldn't fire; the mag drop that couldn't be found; the compass that wouldn't swing; the one engine that always overheated; the controls that couldn't be trimmed .... All of these faults – faults that couldn't be rectified, even after hours of work – were deemed to be caused by bloody Gremlins.

Bill Hooper, the originator of Percy Prune and cartoonist for that masterpiece of humour, *Tee Emm*, produced a drawing of a Gremlin back in 1943. It was an instant success and faithfully reproduced throughout the wartime air forces. A likeness graced many a bomber's nose.

According to Hooper, a squadron serving in India in the 1920s had had a succession of unaccountable setbacks, including at least one forced landing. Gremlins were born right there – at the bar of the mess. The name was a play on the brand name of the only beer available in that outpost: ''Fremlin's'' bottled beer.

Testing, Testing

The A.V. Roe Company built only 300 Mark II Lancasters during the war, and they really would have preferred not to have built any. It was the Air Ministry who insisted that a Bristol Siddeley "Hercules" model should be produced. Their order wasn't viewed with any real interest by A.V. Roe, who were traditionally Rolls Royce minded.

At the time I was working for Bristol, manufacturer of the radial Hercules, and they asked me to do the installation of the four engines on the prototype Lancaster. They did mention to me that it might be something of a difficult assignment.

It proved to be all of that – in fact it became one long continuous battle between the constructors and the engine company. At all times, each wanted to be able to say that they were on schedule and well in front of the other. The gearboxes were a particular headache. First, they were delivered to us late. Then, when they eventually arrived, I spent long hours mounting them on the bulkheads behind the engines, coupling the self-aligning drive shafts, and fitting the hydraulic pumps, generators, and other accessories.

A.V. Roe's chief test pilot was Bill Thorne, who did all the initial Lancaster testing and who spent a great deal of time in the cockpit with me during instrumentation checks. The chief designer was the famous Sir Roy Chadwick, who had been knighted for his development of the Lancaster bomber. They were, of course, both heavily involved in the development of the Mark II.

When the four Hercules engines were finally fitted and mounted I did the flight clearance checks out on the tarmac in one hour.

"Ready?" Bill Thorne's question was loaded with complete disbelief. He jumped into the cockpit with me and the queries came like machine gun bullets: Boost? RPM? Oil pressures? Temperatures? I got out of the Lanc and he literally took off from the hangar apron.

The cafeteria was deserted and I was thankful to sprawl back with a cup of coffee. I was still there when the aircraft came back and parked on the tarmac. In walked Sir Roy – and I braced myself for a shower of complaints.

He came over to my table, sat down, and without a word wrote me out a cheque for ten pounds. So very confidential and under the table ... but I began to think maybe A.V. Roe and I were getting somewhere after all!

It was just a few years later that Sir Roy and Bill Thorne were killed flying an AVRO Tudor over at Woodford.

* * *

Boscombe Down was the scene of more testing than any other airfield in the British Isles. With so many trials of equipment and procedures, and so many prototypes being flown, there was something completely unrehearsed going on all the time.

Bomber aircraft, when engaged in full bomb load trials, were loaded with cement bombs. There was a restricted area on the far side of the field where these dummies could be dropped before landing the bomber. But the area was not always used.

One day, I stood with some others and watched an airman riding his bicycle along the perimeter track just outside the dropping area. All at once he began to pedal like a maniac, as concrete bombs began hitting the ground all around him, too close for anyone's comfort. On another occasion, an early release of a cement bomb tore through a butcher's shop in Amesbury High Street, adjacent to the airfield.

It seemed hardly a day went by without a spectacular crash of some sort. Once, a Mosquito had its port engine cut out on takeoff. Ahead of it were two Blenheim aircraft parked and unattended. The Mossie hit the port wing of the first aircraft and slewed it around, then went under the port wing of the second Blenheim, taking away its port wheel assembly and leaving it leaning on its wing tip. The Mossie proceeded on a few hundred yards, scattering pieces of airframe right and left, until the remains slewed around sharply and disappeared out of sight behind two haystacks.

We all ran up to the expected scene of gore and misery to find that all that was left of the Mossie was the front end. There was not even a floor in the cockpit. The blokes concerned, who had just looked the devil in the face, were outside dusting themselves off. They couldn't have cared less.

Such was the spirit of "Live for the Day."

*   *   *

In service jargon it was a prototype. Let us call it the AS-45: a two-seater trainer of wooden monocoque construction. It had enclosed tandem cockpits and a 600 horsepower radial on the front. That engine was my pigeon. Installation work, ground running, clearance for flight, and initial trials were my responsibility.

The pilot took an instant dislike to the plane, instinctively and for purely non-technical reasons. He did, however, indicate to me on one occasion that it was *not* a stable aircraft. We were flying straight

"YOU AIN'T SEEN NUTHIN' YET, THAT'S JUST OUR P.R.O., ...
WAIT TILL YOU SEE OUR PADRE !"

and level when he turned back to me and raised both hands, indicating "hands off." The machine slowly rolled over on its back.

We were in the initial stages of flight characteristics and handling. The time ticked by – nearly two weeks of it – while we waited for a patch of clear weather in order to do a performance climb to 18,000 feet. Finally, a scrap of blue sky appeared, and we took off. I had pyrometers in the rear cockpit covering cylinder temperatures, and other instruments recording conditions through each 1,000 feet of altitude.

When we pulled out of the top of the climb I noted that my entries in the log had been turning into a laborious scrawl ever since 15,000 feet. It was the first time I had been to 18,000 feet without oxygen, but I was still alert enough at that point to see that the climb record was aborted by high cylinder temperatures. Possibly, it was a cowling fault. We considered that there was time to get down, refuel, and do a repeat while the precious patch of blue sky still held good. With that decision made, the nose went down in a steep dive.

It was not my business to comment on the flying: that was the pilot's job. I watched as the dive steepened. The airspeed indicator moved up to 300 MPH and the hangars down below grew uncomfortably large before he pulled out, circled, and came in for a landing. No panic. I just didn't like it.

With parachutes still on, we waited while the fuel went in. The next few minutes beggared description. I was in the rear cockpit hurrying into my harness while the pilot in front – as he told me later – was doing the same thing, heaving to some extent on the control stick for leverage as he checked his own harness for security. Suddenly he turned around to me. "For Christ's sake, look at this!" he yelled. He was waving the stick above his head.

Later inspection confirmed that a fatigue crack had propagated slightly more than halfway around the tubular base of the control column before final fracture. There were other faults not of much interest – although they were enough to put the AS-45 out to grass without any nostalgia. From either me or the pilot.

But the episode left me with a twinge of philosophic reflection. There was still a future ahead. It was not my time yet.

* * *

I was a carpenter/rigger on No. 10 Bomber Reconnaissance squadron, which flew for a time from Halifax airport at Chibucto and Bayers

Road. When the American Lend-Lease program started we got DB-18A's, which we called Douglas Digbys.

The time was early 1940, and all the workshops were under canvas, without even a hangar. All of us erks boarded in private homes. During the summer a hangar was built at Dartmouth and we trucked back and forth daily. It was a feverish time for everybody. When the Digbys finally arrived we shipped the Wapitis off to St. Thomas for training purposes, and got ourselves checked out as part of a regular crew (airframe/air gunner).

One morning, about 0300 hours, a fellow erk who had more experience on the Digby than I had was showing me how to do a Daily Inspection. When it came time to do a check of the bomb doors he said he'd show me a short-cut.

"Normally," he told me, "you'd move this lever into the open position and then pump like hell on this hydraulic hand pump to get the doors to open. But that's a hell of a lot of work. Now, the trick is to just pull this 'bomb release' lever which works automatically from the hydraulic header tank. Just be careful," he cautioned, "that you only pull the lever down one notch – that's all you need to test the doors."

Being anxious to learn and do something myself I carefully selected what I thought was "one notch." There was a quiet swish and then a hell of a thump. We both bailed out of the aircraft like a streak to find two 500 pound bombs lying between the wheels.

With the help of two understanding armourers and some sweat we got the bombs back up on their racks, and the "Outer Anti-Submarine Patrol" took off as scheduled.

*   *   *

And then there was the Canso, Catalina, PBY, call-it-what-you-will aircraft, that along with the Sunderland and the Liberator did yeoman's service over the seven seas on submarine patrols. Those long, long, boring flights, sometimes more than a day long …. The hour after hour of staring at the glaring ocean, until crews saw mirages and hardly ever the tiny periscopes they were looking for.

But convoy duty, when the aircraft circled and circled the huge ship convoys across the North Atlantic, was just as boring – except when it was brightened by the navy. One Canso circled a convoy for twenty straight hours before the navy shot it down.

*   *   *

Until the Comet jet liner was purchased, the C-5 aircraft was the pride of the RCAF's peacetime fleet of VIP aircraft. It was in reality a DC-4 fuselage with special engines. It was the first RCAF aircraft to have reversible propellers, so that it could be backed up on the ground under its own power – something that always amazed control tower operators who encountered it for the first time.

"Tower, this is Air Force 10,000. Permission to back into the ramp. Over."

An amused and sarcastic controller would drawl. "Air Force 10,000, sure thing. You are cleared to back into the ramp and right through the hangar. Over."

"Roger, tower, Air Force 10,000 backing to the ramp. Out."

Often the astounded controller would be so startled that he would press his mike button as he blurted to his fellow tower workers: "Christ, he's really backing that aircraft up. What in hell is going on – that's impossible!"

Of course, the C-5 crews were always alert for those impromptu broadcasts and did their best to promote them.

* * *

Then there was the Bristol Freighter, an aircraft so homely and awkward-looking it could only have been built in Britain. A huge, fixed undercarriage hung below this sawed-off ugly duckling. The wing resembled a plank torn off a barn, and the entire apparition moved sedately through the air at a galloping 150 miles an hour.

One control tower operator, amazed on first spying one of these aircraft attempting to land on his airfield, called the pilot and asked: "What kind of aircraft is that?"

"A Bristol Freighter," the pilot answered.

To which the controller replied: "Did you make it yourself?"

* * *

A gang of pilots and navigators, CF-100 crews, were sitting around shooting the breeze in the crew room at St. Hubert late one summer afternoon. Suddenly, a pilot rushed in and said a Delta 102 aircraft had just landed.

The crew room erupted. We all piled outside to see this newest of United States Air Force all-weather interceptors – the latest and hottest aircraft in the NORAD inventory. None of us had ever seen one up close.

We stood in a mob as the pilot taxied in and shut down. The 102 seemed to dwarf our CF-100's parked alongside. Its sharply swept back wings formed the Delta shape for which the aircraft was named. Impressive.

Even more impressive was the huge black man who climbed out of the pilot's seat. We all escorted him into the flight room while he did his best to field the volleys of questions we were asking about the 102.

When things settled down he introduced himself. Major "Chappie" James, United States Air Force: the same guy who years later would be chosen to run the entire NORAD command as General James. He had an easy-going manner, and it was soon obvious he was enjoying himself. A navigator asked him about all the latest sophisticated radar and navigation equipment, the "black boxes" that were carried aboard the 102.

"I hear," said the navigator, "that the 102 has some new and powerful black boxes .... "

Chappie James looked him in the eye and replied, "The only black box in that aircraft that works is me."

*   *   *

When the RCAF's Air Division in Europe was re-equipping with CF-104 Super Starfighters in 1962, they were the hottest aircraft flying anywhere.

Everyone was curious about their performance, and tales of their Mach 2 speed had preceded them into squadron service. It was a deadly thing to look at, for its wings resembled a pair of razor blades. In reality, it was a flying engine, a very powerful engine, and when that engine quit the aircraft came down like a brick and at the same gliding angle. Whenever the groundcrew ran the engine to full power they literally had to chain the aircraft down. The horrendous ear-splitting noise sounded like a moose being goosed by a locomotive.

Someone asked one of the pilots about the tremendous acceleration on takeoff. "Does it really take off that fast?" he asked.

"Fast?" the pilot said. "Fast? It's the only aircraft I've flown where my foreskin rolls back on takeoff."

*   *   *

When the RCAF began flying the F-86 Sabre jet it caused all kinds of interest and a few problems.

The F-86 couldn't exceed the speed of sound in level flight, but put it into a vertical dive and hold it there and *boom!* the sound wave broke loose and struck the ground. Phones rang, babies cried, mothers and old folks panicked, and windows were often broken. Some of the experienced Sabre jockeys became so proficient they could aim the "boom." They climbed the jet to 40,000 feet, flew over their "target," rolled the plane over, and pulled it through in a vertical dive.

Orders were issued. No pilots were to exceed the speed of sound over built-up areas. Since the press were constantly confusing any ground explosion with a sonic boom they added to the general clamour for the air force to cease and desist.

One astute radio announcer decided to capitalize on the national interest by recording a sonic boom. He came to Ottawa with two Auxiliary jet squadrons from Vancouver as part of their summer camp. He asked me to organize a flight with a Sabre pilot while he got his recording equipment into position at the south end of the Uplands airfield.

The Auxiliary pilot tried for two days but we never once heard a boom. We could follow the F-86 with binoculars as it crossed the field at 40,000 feet. (Often vapour trails made it plainly visible, and we were able to follow it without the glasses.) When it got overhead, the radio announcer would begin his running commentary and describe what was happening as the pilot rolled over and headed down. We could see a tiny streak of vapour as he passed through the barrier, and the announcer's voice would rise to a crescendo: "And here it comes, ladies and gentlemen! The first sonic boom ever recorded."

We never heard a thing. We finally reached the conclusion that the pilot wasn't achieving a completely vertical descent and that the sound waves were thus angled away from us.

Not to worry. Our brave announcer found a large tin wash basin and a baseball bat. On cue, when he reached the exciting climax of his spiel, I banged the bat on the wash basin.

*   *   *

When the RCAF Air Division re-equipped with new Marks of F-86 Sabre jets, the old jets were given off to Turkey. A couple of RCAF jet pilots were sent to Eskisehir in Turkey to check out the Turkish Air Force pilots.

The checkout system was simple. A Turkish pilot sat at the controls ready to fly. An RCAF pilot stood beside him on one wing, while a

Turkish pilot who could speak English stood on the other wing. Whatever the Canadian on wing A told the Turk on wing B was relayed to the guy in the cockpit. When everyone ran out of instructions and questions the pilot took off. The system seemed to work.

Meanwhile, loads of spare parts and ground handling equipment were being flown into Eskisehir by North Star transports. The first arrival was nerve wracking, since the Turkish control tower refused to reply to calls for landing instructions. The North Star circled and circled the field, calling and calling, until out of necessity it landed. The irate Captain climbed the tower stairs to have a word with the controller. He found a young Turkish officer sitting there with a handful of cards on which were written various landing instructions in the English language. When the Captain demanded to know why the controller hadn't used the instructions he replied, in halting English, that he was too shy to try his English over the radio.

Still remembered about that trip: the billions and billions of flys; the staggering heat; the hundreds of old military aircraft of every make parked everywhere around the airfield; the lack of toilet paper and the running faucet in lieu of; the American Travellers cheques we couldn't cash until we got to Ankara and found the Canadian Counsel; the model A Ford truck that delivered the barrel of oil for the North Star's engines; the first question asked of the RCAF technical officer, "How do you drain the fuel from a Sabre jet?" – and his reply, "Start the engine and burn it off."

The fact that nothing could be arranged, no decision taken, until the problem had been passed up to the most senior officer on the base, was equally unforgettable. And then there was the Turkish officer who said to us, "Next time you come, bring elastics." We had him repeat that sentence over and over again. But we couldn't make any sense of "elastics" until he walked over and kicked the tires on our aircraft.

Most memorable of all was the flight out of Turkey, when we arrived over Italy and the Italian air controllers called and wanted to know who we were and where we came from. Our little Turkish friend in the control tower at Eskisehir had forgotten to pass the flight plan we had so carefully filed with him.

Around the World

We sailed for overseas on the *Louis Pasteur*, a renowned old tub that carried thousands of Canadians to war. Very conscious of the possibility of being torpedoed by a German sub I was alert for any danger. One evening, when I heard a loud explosion from the rear deck, I just about fainted with fear. I began running for the open deck while pulling on my life preserver. A friend stopped me and calmed me down. We hadn't been hit by a torpedo, he explained. The explosion had been a practice firing of one of our own guns.

*   *   *

In India, in 1945, the Japanese were being pushed back from northern Burma, and our short trips began getting longer and longer. We were flying Liberators, and they didn't have an Elsan – but there was a tube up front for urination purposes. This was used quite frequently, and it caused my rear turret to glaze over. I hated cleaning the piss off it after each trip.

To solve the problem I got two .50 calibre ammunition tins and placed them in the waist position of the aircraft. They made excellent toilets. I would dump them overboard on the way home.

One day I decided that since we were getting so much shit from the Japs over the target it would only be right if I gave them back a little. From then on, whenever the bomb aimer called, "Bombs away!" I would dash out of my turret, open the hatch, and dump the cans. Back in my turret I'd yell over the intercom: "Shit's away – let's go home."

Of course I never did this if enemy aircraft were around. Then, I had to wait for a safer moment. But I've always wondered what the reaction was down below when those cans hit the deck.

*   *   *

In the days when the No. 1 Air Division consisted of twelve squadrons of Sabre jets, the RCAF was the hottest air force in Europe. They proved it time after time. Each year, in June, the cream of the various NATO air forces flew into the Royal Netherlands Air Force base at Leeuwarden to compete for the coveted Guynemer Trophy. For four straight years, from 1958 to 1961, the RCAF won that aerial gunnery championship flying their Canadian-built F-86's.

All of the NATO air forces were eligible to compete for the trophy, but not all of them rose to the challenge each year. The French always

indicated that they would enter, but only showed up the first year – when they came dead last. (This was just a few years before General De Gaulle threw all NATO forces out of France.) The RAF usually entered; but the United States Air Force only participated once – when it came last in a six nation event in 1959.

When the RCAF won its fourth straight victory in 1961 it was competing against Belgium, the Netherlands, Denmark, Germany, Norway, and Italy. The countries finished in exactly that order.

Competition for a place on the RCAF's four man, one spare, team was fierce. A month's hard practice at the air gunnery range in Decimomanu, Sardinia, was necessary to sort out our best marksmen. It was also the place where the cream of the groundcrew was chosen. While it was a test of aerial marksmanship for the fighter pilots, the event was also a real competition between groundcrews. Winning meant having the most reliable aircraft, and the RCAF groundcrews worked like demons to harmonize the six .5 machine guns in the nose of each Sabre and to keep each radar gun sight tuned to perfection. The administrative types (like myself), who were included in the yearly event were not given training of any kind. Which turned out to be a sad oversight in that year of 1961.

It soon became clear that the Canadian attitude towards winning didn't extend to other nationalities. The Italians spent most of their time arguing vociferously with everyone about the rules – the mixture of languages adding a special flavour and excitement and producing some comic translations. The Germans, with their newly approved military trade unions, downed tools whenever possible; while the Norwegians looked upon the competition as a holiday and made the most of it. This rather lackadaisical attitude among some opponents was compounded by various nationalistic interpretations of the rules. Since the RCAF had now won three competitions in a row, it was implied that perhaps the Canadians might be bending these rules in some way.

One of the cardinal rules of the competition declared that all aircraft had to be lined up in an exact order in front of the hangars each morning. They had to start the day in that position, and they had to be in exactly the same order when the day's shooting was completed. Everything in full view, please. Our RCAF groundcrew went to great lengths to exploit the situation, since they knew that they were being watched like hawks by the competition, who were trying to find some technique that would account for the Canadian success. Late each afternoon our groundcrew gave one "secret" away.

One ploy was to cover the radome on the nose of the Sabre with aluminum foil. When our allies saw the five Canadian Sabres so adorned it took less than an hour for all aircraft to have their noses taped over with foil. Thirty-five jets all in a row, with foil on their noses – and more than thirty-five explanations in seven languages to justify the reason.

The merriment of our groundcrew knew no bounds. They peered from their hangar windows watching with glee as first the Germans and then all competitors rushed to emulate the Canadians. When our groundcrew grew tired of taping on foil and left their Sabres bare one evening, all other aircraft were also swiftly denuded.

Next, some RCAF type decided to place a pail about six feet in front of each aircraft. Then he ran a heavy chain from the nose wheel, along the tarmac, and into the bucket. When all five RCAF Sabres were so adorned the groundcrew gathered inside the hangar to wait. Reaction came immediately. Each competing jet suddenly sprouted a chain and pail in exactly the same arrangement.

Scores from each day's shooting were posted on a large scoreboard for all to see. This was after each metal-meshed drogue (or flag, as the pilots called it), was carefully examined by an official panel of judges chosen from various countries. Each contestant used a different coloured bullet or shell, which left its colour around the hole when it penetrated the drogue. It may have been that they hadn't checked the judges for colour blindness. Either that, or nationalistic fervour rising to the occasion, was responsible for the long and endless arguments between judges and pilots.

Actually, it wasn't necessary to post the scores, for it was quite evident which teams had faired badly on any particular day. Half the German High Command descended on the base on the second day of competition, and loud and public brow beatings were given to the hapless German team. National pride was at stake – although the Norwegians and Italians didn't seem to notice. They were rarely around when the scores were tabulated and only got back when the morning's work began.

Meanwhile, the RCAF supernumerary personnel like myself, who were in attendance for various administrative purposes, were having our own competition. Our group of five had registered at a tiny, but beautiful hotel in the town of Leeuwarden. There the battle of the nationalities continued, albeit in a more subtle fashion.

Leeuwarden, at that time a town of about 60,000, had been liberated by the Canadian Army in 1945; and while I knew this, I hadn't realized what it would mean to show up in Holland wearing a Canadian uniform.

Our initiation began the moment the five of us tried to register at the desk in the small lobby. Mine Host, a huge Dutchman with an equally large cigar, descended upon us to give his personal greeting. It turned out that he owned not only the hotel, but the world's supply of De Kuyper gin. A lot of Canadian Army veterans no doubt remember that variety of white lightning. Not so our RCAF group, who had arrived in Holland dragging many duty-free forty pounders of Canadian rye whiskey.

Although we wanted to take our luggage to our rooms, our host insisted that we should have a drink. While we had been signing the register he had been busy at the bar that ran the length of the lobby, lining up a row of large glasses and filling them with a whitish fluid. When we asked what it was, he looked at us blankly before informing us that it was gin.

"Your health, gentlemen," he said, and downed his drink in one gulp. We five followed suit, although it took many swallows, interspersed with racking coughs, before we drained our glasses. It made my eyes water (and as far as I could ever tell that was the only water in the place). We'd barely emptied our glasses before he filled them again – and the party was underway.

This set the pattern for the remainder of our stay. When we arrived at the hotel each evening our host was waiting patiently. The glasses, charged to the brim, were also waiting. We were not permitted to pay for a drink. Our only obligation was to keep pace with our host – drink for drink.

There was no escape. The only entrance to the hotel lay past the bar, which also blocked the stairs to our rooms – and our beaming host was determined to single-handedly repay Canada for the liberation of his country. Most of us never did get an evening meal. And the duty-free quarts of rye we had carefully carried to Holland stood forlornly in our rooms.

One rainy day, when flying was washed out, our host decided to show us the local countryside. He packed the five of us into his tiny Daf, a Dutch built car not sold outside Holland. He drove like he drank – flat out and carefree – even though the roads in that northern area of Holland were very narrow and built high upon the dikes separating the various canals and ditches. Ignoring the rain, arms waving and hands pointing, he gave us a running description of where and how the Canadians had driven out the Germans.

It was a memorable, if hair-raising ride, and it culminated in a visit to a Dutch pottery works. There our host proudly showed us the special techniques that had been used to make a commemorative, limited edition of plates depicting the insignia of each Canadian unit that had taken part in the liberation. His hotel lobby was decorated with a complete set of these plates, and he spent hours telling and retelling the history of each unit and its particular part in those long ago battles.

As the competition neared an end and we began making preparations to return to France, our host grew alarmed. He doubled his hospitality. This doubled our embarrassment and obligation, and we decided to try and return some of his kindness. (Our decision, however, may have been prompted by a collective longing for a drink of our national beverage.)

On the last evening, instead of accepting his gin when we returned to the hotel, we coaxed our host upstairs to a gathering held in my room. Out came the many bottles of rye, a drink our host professed never to have tasted. I gave him a large tumbler that would hold at least twelve ounces. "Say when," I directed, as he held the glass and I poured. I hesitated when the glass was two-thirds full but he waved at me to continue. I asked if he wanted water and he replied no and gave me a funny look. So I filled his glass to the brim and we all said cheers or something. Our host drained his portion in one great swallow, smiled, wiped his lips, and thrust out his glass for more.

"It's goot, yah," he said, nodding and smiling. "Canadian, yah, goot."

To our amazement it took three glasses before he fell backward in his chair and began snoring. With great delight we all hoisted him aloft, carrying him upstairs to his apartment and a very puzzled wife.

All things considered it was a very successful gunnery competition: RCAF pilots won their fourth straight Guynemer Trophy; RCAF ground-crew gleefully won their battle of wits; and RCAF hangers-on figured their drinking contest was at least a draw.

Although there are those who feel we should have been awarded the De Kuyper Trophy.

*　　*　　*

I was serving with the RCAF's 115 Air Transport Unit at El Arish. It was part of the United Nations Emergency Force (UNEF), and our air-field was about an hour's drive from the town of Gaza, where the UNEF Headquarters was located.

The road to Gaza lay over and through and around the shifting sand dunes of the desert, and often you would catch a glimpse of tents in the distance as you roared along in your jeep. The tents belonged to the

212

Bedouins, the nomad Arab tribes who were continually on the move with their herds of goats, sheep, and camels. They seldom stayed more than a few days in any one location. Their frayed and patched tents would appear suddenly on the horizon, and just as suddenly and as silently they would later disappear. There was never any contact between the RCAF and the tribesmen.

One day, alone in the jeep on the way to town, I spotted an Arab boy standing back off the road. As I passed he made a smoking gesture with his hand. I stopped the jeep and motioned for him to come forward, but he didn't move. He continued to make the smoking gesture, putting his hand to his mouth and pretending to puff.

Taking out my half-finished pack of cigarettes, I threw it on the sand towards the boy. He was only about ten or twelve years of age, and I guessed that he wanted the cigarettes for his father or for trading purposes. Poised for flight like a frightened deer, he didn't come any closer. But as I drove on I looked back to see him leap forward and retrieve the cigarettes. Then he darted away over the desert towards some Arab tents that I could glimpse in the distance.

I made a mental note of just where I had thrown the cigarettes, and a few days later I drove out with some candy bars. I found a place nearby where a piece of the roadway had been undercut, and in this ideal hiding place I left the candy. There was no one in sight.

The next day I had to make another trip to Gaza, and again I took some candy along. When I reached into the hiding place under the edge of the roadway, I found two tiny birds' eggs. I looked around quickly, but there was no one for miles. Taking the tiny eggs, I replaced them with the candy.

After that I made regular trips out to the cache, each time taking candy bars. Often there would be birds' eggs in return, but sometimes there was nothing. Once there was a broken, but shiny, zipper. In the three or four weeks in which I made almost daily visits to our secret hiding place I never once saw the young boy.

Then one day, when I reached expectantly under the ledge to see what had been left for me, I found my own candy bars. I stood up quickly and looked in the direction of the nomad camp. There was nothing to be seen but sand.

*   *   *

RCAF Station Goose Bay in Labrador, like other air force units in remote northern areas, tried to help any civilians living nearby. The local inhabitants lived for the most part in unfederated villages. The one near Goose Bay was called Happy Valley. It may well be a modern city today, but in the early days of Goose Bay the civilians were fairly nomadic and, of course, very rugged and individualistic characters.

The air force Doctor had asked a Newfoundland man to leave a urine sample and to call back in a few days for the results. The Doctor was very busy that week, and by the time the Newfoundlander returned he had forgotten where he had placed the test results.

"It's here somewhere," the Doctor muttered, rummaging in the papers on his desk. "Oh, yes, here it is." He picked up a card. "It says there was blood, albumen, pus, and serum."

The Newfoundlander interrupted. "Jesus, Doc," he said, "was there no piss in it at all?"

* * *

Another time, an air force Doctor was taking a history from his Newfoundlander patient.

"Is your father alive?"

"No, Doc."

"What did he die of?"

"I don't rightly know, Doc, but I think it was cancer."

"Is your mother living?"

"No, she died."

"What did she die of?"

"I don't know Doc, but it was nothin' serious."

* * *

We were stationed at Rivers, Manitoba, when the air force introduced gliders into the service. It was winter time and brother was it cold on those old prairies! The temperature sat at thirty below zero for days at a stretch – but the flying went on. Gliders were being towed around every day. Quite a sight if you've never seen them before.

Most Saturdays, a lot of our gang of airmen would head for town and the local beer parlour. We'd sit and drink draft beer with the local farmers who came to town on Saturday to shop. After our first week of towing gliders, a farmer landed at our table. "Well," he said, "I see you air force fellars are no smarter than us farmers."

"How's that?" we all asked.

"I seen you all week trying to start your airplanes. Towing them all over the sky, and you still couldn't start them. Just like I did with my old tractor. Too cold to start anythin' this week."

*   *   *

In the early 1960s, while serving as a navigator with 408 squadron, I made a number of flights as part of a Canadian courtesy crew aboard Soviet aircraft. We were shuttling between Moscow and Havana, with *en route* stops at Prestwick and Gander.

The USSR was not yet a member of the International Civil Aviation Organization, and we were aboard to ensure that flight and safety regulations were observed. This was a delicate task in view of the fact that the Soviet crew spoke not a word of English (at least, that is what we were told). On board the Ilyushin 18 turboprop, on my first trip, was Major Yuri Gagarin. The world's first man in space was making a goodwill trip to Cuba.

All went well until we landed in Gander for refuelling. Through a bureaucratic foul-up, airport officials demanded payment of the Soviet Captain – in cash – to cover landing fees and the 5,213 gallons of fuel he had taken aboard. A great deal of hand waving, hand wringing, and shouting in two languages took place; and the whole thing was building into an international incident when a Canadian airport official approached me with a solution.

"Y'got a Shell credit card, Air Force?"

"Well, yes, but – "

"The only way you're getting that bird off the ground is to cough up for all that juice, and since none of you has the cash .... "

"How much cash?" I asked.

"Two thousand one hundred and thirty-seven dollars."

"Oh, my God!"

"And thirty-two cents."

He didn't even smile.

How in hell, I thought, was I going to convince my wife that a gasoline bill for $2,137.32 was for our Volkswagen Beetle?

Desperate, we finally convinced the fellow in charge to phone Shell Headquarters in Toronto for guidance. In the end we got our man to Havana in time to meet the waiting Mr. Castro, the Soviets salvaged their pride – and my Shell credit card remained inviolate.

216

Vive la France!

Our learned people at the Department of External Affairs talk in terms of cultural shock when they discuss what happens to an English-speaking Canadian family, thrust into the innards of a European community. Our military leaders dismiss the subject as frivolous, if they think of it at all. It has been many years since my RCAF tour of duty in France with Canada's NATO forces, but I still have the mental scars to prove they should give the subject some thought. Four years can be a long time anywhere. Living in France with young children is a very long time. Let me explain.

We arrived, my wife and I and our four children, late on a Saturday night in the town of Metz, France, located near the German border. The RCAF had booked the six of us into a small hotel across the street from the railway station. The two large, if antiquated, hotel rooms were our first French home: four children in one room, the parents in an adjoining room. Exhausted by the long train ride from Le Havre, we all went immediately to bed.

We arose on Sunday with everyone starving. "The railway stations have the best food in France," I declared, the bold statement based on former conversations with veteran NATO troops. To my surprise it was accepted at face value, and we proceeded that Sunday noon to march *en masse* from our hotel to the station.

Sunday in France is eat-out-day. We learned this upon entering a tremendous hall that held a minimum of 500 diners, all of them busy at their meals. Waiters flew about the huge room balancing overloaded trays, and the noise that arose from the excited conversations and rattling of dishes echoed off the bare brick walls. I think we were all intimidated as we paused, wondering how to proceed. I know I was.

A *maitre d'* finally bustled up, and with bows and *bonjours* escorted us into the middle of the pack. I had barely sat down before a chorus of, "I want a hamburger and fries and hot dogs and malted milkshakes and Cokes," started. When the shouting had subsided I launched into the first of my four-year series of dining-out lectures.

"In France they do not have hamburgs or hot dogs. They do not have ketchup or Cokes. They do not have milkshakes or pizza." Those were only the gut words. There were others.

The children's rebuttal of, "What *do* they have?" sent me into the giant French menu. With much difficulty I translated: snails, onion soup, quiche, pork .... I could find nothing they liked except steak.

"How would you all like steak, french fries, and salad?" Agreed. "Eating out with this gang is going to cost me," I told my wife.

221

"Well, at least it makes the ordering easier," she replied.

Since none of us could speak the language I thought I did fairly well in communicating what we wanted for we received everything we ordered in a few minutes. Oh, sure, the milk was a problem. The children complained that it was warm and didn't taste like milk. This gave me a chance to launch into the second instalment of my lecture series: Living In France Is Different.

As the meal progressed, I noticed that my wife didn't appear to be enjoying hers. I asked if something was wrong, and she gestured towards the next table. There, at a table for eight, was a very noisy French family of six adults and two poodles. All had chairs and all had place settings and all had large white napkins knotted around their necks. Except the poodles had bowls rather than plates.

"*Vive la France*," I said. "Pay no attention."

Things settled down and I began to look around myself. Relaxing for the first time, I started to enjoy the scene. A babble of French hung over everything as waiters popped corks and flames leaped over chafing dishes. I sat marvelling at the skill and ease with which the waiters manoeuvred through the crowded room, their great platters held overhead.

"I wonder where the washroom is?"

The question brought me back to the practicalities of family living. "I'll ask the waiter," I told my wife. "Watch this .... " I caught a passing waiter by the elbow, "*Monsieur. Où est la toilette?*"

"*Toute la droite*," he replied, pointing directly across the room.

"*Merci beaucoup*," I thanked him, and then waited for the applause from my wife for my continental flair, my flawless performance in French. But she had already departed – hurrying in the direction of the waiter's pointed finger.

With my ego sufficiently fed, I began to feel expansive. Another bottle of wine might be appropriate to the moment. My wife reappeared as soon as I had picked up the wine list. She looked flushed and upset.

"Did you find it okay? I was just going to order another bottle of –"

"I didn't go!" she hissed at me. "My Gawd, you should *see* that place. Men and women are using the same toilet. A man held the door open for me. He was zipping up his pants!"

"So what? You have to remember that we are in France. They do things differently. You'll get used to it."

"But you don't understand! They don't have toilets. Just holes in the floor. Men and women are squatting over those holes, side by side, and some of them are talking to each other."

222

"Maybe," I laughed, "they are married couples."

"Come on, let's get back to our hotel. Hurry up you kids and finish your ice cream," she directed. "Get the check," she demanded of me.

"Watch this," I said. "Talk about catching on fast. Watch me get the check. No one would believe this is our first day in France." I caught a waiter's eye. "*Monsieur. L'addition s'il vous plaît.*"

"*Oui, immédiatement.*"

"How was that?" I beamed across the table.

"Oh, come on! You can practise your stupid French later. Honey, I have to go," she begged.

"Take it easy, take it easy, the waiter will only be a second."

I scrutinized the bill presented by the waiter, which looked like a long laundry list. I recognized a printed phrase, "*Service complet,*" which signified that the tip was included in the total. Still, a small tip would be appropriate. It would set us up for future dinners since the restaurant was handy to the hotel.

I reached for my wallet and the fistful of franc notes I would need – only to discover that I didn't *have* a wallet.

"You don't have my wallet, do you?" I inquired of the desperate woman now standing across the table from me.

"Oh, for God's sake, don't tell me you've lost your wallet!" she yelled.

"Well, it's not here," I said, searching under my chair. I looked up to see three waiters where one had stood a moment ago. The room seemed to have grown quiet. It was then that any small number of French words I thought I knew deserted me. "I can't find my wallet," I said in English to the waiters.

"*Comment?*" they asked.

I rediscovered some French words: "*Francs, pas francs.*" I shrugged, waved my hands. Finally I reached into my back pocket where the wallet should have been and turned it inside out. None of this helped.

The *maitre d'* arrived, followed by a phalanx of waiters. People were standing, our kids were dipping their bread into their water glasses and throwing it at each other. I collected myself and addressed the *maitre d'* in English. "I have left my wallet at the hotel. I will go and get it."

He understood. I couldn't believe it. He understood.

"*Oui, monsieur,*" he said. "*D'accord.*"

With my wife well in the lead we wove our way through the interested patrons and started across the street to the hotel. When I turned to hustle the kids along I found four aproned waiters immediately behind me, grimly marching in our procession.

The hotel manager appeared alarmed as our group suddenly possessed his small lobby. "*Monsieur*," he inquired, "what is the matter?" I explained that I had left my money in my room and was coming back for it to pay for our meal.

He turned immediately to a waiter. "*Combien?*" The waiter produced the check with a flourish. "*Moment*," said the manager. And going to his cash drawer he drew out some franc notes and paid our bill.

"I could kiss this guy," I said to my wife.

But there was no wife. She had disappeared upstairs.

Bienvenue au France.

* * *

When wearing your Canadian uniform in France you often drew curious stares from the French citizens. This resulted in one being overly conscious of one's deportment when in public places. I guess we were all fearful of making a *gaucherie* that would reflect poorly on Canadians and Canada.

Looking back, I feel we must have provided the French with unlimited dinner stories or at least humorous office chatter. While our actions, for the most part, were innocent enough, in hindsight they were remarkably stupid. It was the language of course, or lack of it, that caused the now laughable incidents. My first and last bus ride in the town of Metz was a classic case.

One morning, *sans* car, I had to take a city bus to the railway station, where I could catch the air force bus to the air base. I didn't know the amount of the fare, and didn't know how to ask, so I put several coins in my hand and crowded aboard. The bus driver looked at me. "*Oui?*" he asked.

"*La guerre*," I said, holding out my money.

The driver stopped the bus, and the passengers all tuned in. "*Comment?*" he inquired.

"*La guerre*," I repeated, loudly, thinking he hadn't heard me.

Never changing the expression on his face, the bus driver continued to look me up and down, as though admiring my uniform. "*La guerre?*" he questioned.

"*Oui*," I murmured, becoming less sure of myself and thrusting the money at him.

"*Monsieur, c'est la gare.*" And with quiet dignity he took a franc from my hand and made change.

Oh, my God! I thought, as I pushed into the crowd of strap hangers.

I'd asked him to take me to the war. I was too mortified to notice if anyone was smiling.

*　　*　　*

In the early days of the Air Division in Metz, circa 1953-54, there were few amenities on the base. Most of the personnel got their jollies in town at the Globe Hotel. A whole gang of airmen would gather there after work. Some, in fact, lived at the Globe.

It was a marvellous spot. There was always some excitement, for it stood across from the railway station and the street held many of the hotels. We would sit on the terrace and drink Amos beer or *vin ordinaire* and amuse ourselves by watching the passing parade (including, of course, those gorgeous French girls).

It was a time of strife for France. The Algerian question of independence was being bitterly disputed, and armed patrols circulated through the town keeping the railway station under constant surveillance. One afternoon two Italian labourers got off the train, cardboard suitcases in hand. They were fresh from Italy and seeking work in construction. Both were squat and swarthy. They were gunned down on the sidewalk almost in front of us by an armed patrol.

The police had been looking for two Algerians of the same build and age for some criminal offence. They didn't bother to ask questions. It was not an isolated incident – late at night in the restaurants, shootings and knifings seemed routine. They provided a free floor show for your late night onion soup.

Algerians were hard pressed to find jobs, and so many were pedlars. One Algerian pedlar we nicknamed "Johnny Goddamn." He was fierce and swarthy-looking and covered in rolled-up rugs, cheap jewellery, neckties, and "filthy postcards." Johnny Goddamn showed up each afternoon to pester every one of us into buying something. In the summer months he was there, as well, to meet the tourist buses that rolled in around six o'clock. Many of these were filled with elderly tourists from Britain who were "off to see the continent."

Although he couldn't speak one word of English before he arrived in France, Johnny Goddamn had picked up some powerful phrases from our constant tutoring. We had all helped increase his vocabulary until it was rich and descriptive.

As soon as a bus pulled up at the hotel, Johnny Goddamn flapped up to it, his rugs and beads flying in the breeze. When the passengers stiffly began to descend he made his sales pitch.

226

"Hello, you goddamn bastards!" he would scream at them. "You fucking assholes want rugs? All goddamn good fucking rugs."

The terrified tourists would put their heads down and scuttle for the safety of the hotel lobby, while Johnny Goddamn ran after them screaming his profanities.

*   *   *

While stationed in France with the RCAF's NATO force, my wife and I received yearly visits from our mothers. These were special occasions, and (if you wished to retain your sanity) they required careful pre-planning. How did you entertain staid, Protestant, English-born-and-raised senior citizens in that most unholy of countries – France?

Air force families with young children already lived under continual cultural shock; French ways were quite different from Canadian ways. The visits of the children's grandparents provided so much comic relief that they actually helped remove our own cultural blinders.

My wife's mother had been raised in the back of an Anglican church, or so it seemed to my more agnostic view. She disliked, to put it mildly, Catholics, the Catholic church, priests, nuns, France, the French language, Liberals, drinking, and smoking. Wine was a separate subject: the very nectar of the devil. Nevertheless, the pull of the grandchildren was such that she could force herself to endure two weeks in hedonistic French society. And those two weeks gave her enough ammunition for a series of Do and Don't letters that lasted for a year. I could always tell when one of her missives had arrived with just one quick look at my wife's face.

"Another letter from mother?" I would ask.

Her tears would start before I could hastily find something to do outside.

To be fair, it wasn't only mother-in-law but my own mother who visited. I don't know where she thought we were living but the entire scene baffled her.

"What are they jabbering about?" she would angrily demand, as we sat at a lovely street-side *bistro*, supposedly enjoying the passing scene.

"Who do you mean?"

"All these people around us. What are they jabbering about?"

"Mother, they are French people."

"I know they're French," she would indignantly reply, "but why don't they speak English?"

"Mother, you are in France. These are French people. They're speaking their own language."

227

"MY FRENCH MUST BE IMPROVING! I THINK SHE WINKED AT ME."

"I know that for goodness sake! But why don't they speak English? All this jabber, jabber, I can't understand a word."

She was English to the core. It made you realize in one quick flash why they lost India.

On one visit, mother brought along a spinster aunt whom she had collected in England. They were both in their late seventies at the time. Their visit coincided with a heat wave, a rarity in France, and the temperature sat at ninety degrees for days. Both of them, it turned out, were wearing undergarments of 100 per cent wool. This information came from my wife who had charge of the laundry.

Nothing we could do (or rather, my wife could do), would get them to stop wearing the long wool drawers and tops. To remove them meant that, as Aunt Martha explained, "We'd catch our death."

Neither drank spirits, preferring their everlasting hot tea. But occasionally, since the children were drinking gallons of soft drinks, they turned their attention to something cooler. Those were the times when I had a chance to serve them champagne, which was less expensive and more readily available than soft drinks. My servings were accompanied by stern warnings that French "soda pop" was different from anything they knew. "It fizzes more," I told them.

With dripping brows and beet-red faces they assured me that that was fine. It didn't take more than one large glass to enlarge their perspective of the world. They would repeat over and over: "France has the very best soda pop!" Often they broke into song and delighted us with, "There's a Long Long Trail A-winding," "It's a Long Long Way to Tipperary," "Pack up Your Troubles in Your Old Kit Bag," and other English wartime tunes.

The singing often took place in the kitchen as they helped with the cleaning up following a meal. They would wave sodden dish cloths around in time to their songs. The kitchen would be awash with kids, dish water, off-tune songs, and much laughter as I opened more champagne to reinforce their merriment.

It didn't take many visits to make my wife and I realize that our relatives weren't as interested in sight-seeing as we thought they would be. The time when we all jammed into the car with mother and Aunt Martha for a weekend excursion was nothing if not educational.

"What is that building they're tearing down?"

"Where?"

Mother pointed from the front seat. "There on the corner. That big stone building."

"That's a sixteenth-century cathedral, mother. Matter of fact, it's an historic landmark and one of the finest churches in France," I said enthusiastically, pleased she had noticed it.

"That old thing? It looks to me like they're tearing it down."

"No, no, the scaffolding is where they are making repairs."

"We have better churches than that in Canada. Far nicer." Mother said this to aunty, who was busy in the back seat reading comic books to the children.

Hotel accommodations always brought the same question: "Why do they have two toilets in the bathrooms?"

My wife got used to that question – but she never learned how to answer it. Choosing and phrasing her words carefully she would attempt, in very delicate language, to imply that the *bidet* was universal throughout France and that all homes and hotels had them.

Then they would both ask: "But what is it for?"

My wife would go over the same ground again, carefully rearranging her words, while they both stood listening and nodding. After one such explanation mother turned to Aunt Martha and said, "That's right. Everything for the men."

Despite myself, I became a fierce defender of everything French, just to remain on an even keel. Everything mother and aunty ate, drank, listened to, or looked at, was related immediately to their own lifestyles, judged, and found wanting.

The strawberries were much larger and sweeter in England. The bread was better in Canada. The buses and trains more efficient in England and Canada. It rained more in France than in England. French beef was tough and the butter tasted rancid and the fish was far fresher in Toronto. The French girls would wear anything to show off their figures, and the French men were ugly little things who smelled of garlic and tobacco. How they reached those judgements without ever meeting one French person left me wondering.

We found that only one attraction in the whole of France pleased them: the military cemeteries. Since we were stationed in Metz it was quite easy to visit Verdun, Luxembourg, and some of the other beautifully cared-for burial grounds. These were moving occasions for all of us. We cherished the moments when we stood silently, tears streaming, in those quiet sanctuaries. It was when we were at the Vimy Memorial that Aunt Martha gave me a new definition of spinsterhood. "You know," she said softly, "none of the boys from our town came back from here."

Since both women had lived through two world wars they had very

230

definite opinions on every nation's military ability. When they chanced to see French military personnel on the streets it activated some hidden store of memories in each of them. Both had minor hearing problems, and their loud conversations, as we strolled about the towns, left me thankful that they couldn't be understood.

"Here, look at these two, aren't they scruffy?" (As they brushed past two soldiers.) "No wonder they couldn't fight the Germans."

If a French soldier hand-in-hand with his girlfriend caught their eye, it brought an immediate reaction. "Did you see that, Maggie?" Aunt Martha would call out in a shrill voice. "Well, I never! Kissing right on the street."

"Well, you know what Frenchmen are like. No telling what they'd be doing if we weren't here."

"Here now, look at this policeman in his fancy cloak." (As a *gendarme* passed, smiling at them.) "Doesn't he look a proper toff!" And they would both stop and stare after the officer.

I gave up trying to explain the French money to them. Especially the exchange rate among francs, dollars, and pounds. It was far easier to pay for anything they wanted to buy – which wasn't much – and much gentler on the nerves. Of course they assumed they would be swindled in every shop.

Shopkeepers were mere servants to do their immediate bidding without question. Being English by birth seemed to have instilled in them a belief that they had only to speak to be understood. On those occasions when they insisted on buying some small things for the children, they aged clerks before your eyes.

"How much is this one?"

"*Pardon, madame?*"

"How much? How much?" Louder and more insistent.

"*Pardon?*"

"HOW MUCH? What's the matter with him?" They would turn to me. "Is he deaf?"

"Mother, he doesn't understand you."

"What do you mean? All I asked was the price."

"Yes, but you're speaking English."

"Well, what's the difference?"

"Here, let me try."

What may have confused them was our RCAF base, where we would take the ladies for sporting events such as bingo. This English-speaking enclave, right in the middle of the French community, may have signified to them that the whole country was really English – with the exception of one or two difficult people scattered here and there.

Mother-in-law added an extra touch with her religious conviction – even though the truth was that one seldom saw a French priest. Although the country was considered Catholic, the populace seemed jaded about church going. Whenever you did glimpse a priest he was usually labouring along on an old bicycle, newspapers peeking out from his habit (insulating material, I was told). Mother-in-law, however, was convinced that every second French person was a working member of the church. It would have taken the Archbishop of Canterbury to persuade her otherwise.

Her approach to living in France was straightforward. She wondered: "Why do you choose to live here? Why don't you come back to Canada where you belong?" The letters which she would begin writing as soon as she herself had arrived back in Canada, would continue that theme. I remember one in particular which summed up all her visits. It contained this sentence, embedded within a list of the latest laundry products my wife should use:

"It seems to me, from my last visit, that France is getting so French."

Northern Lights

In one of his poems, Robert Service said something to the effect that strange things are done in the land of the midnight sun. The RCAF's most northerly base – Resolute Bay on Cornwallis Island, some 1,100 miles due north of Churchill, Manitoba – often bore witness to that saying.

When the RCAF began flying correspondents into its remote bases, a female reporter for the CBC fell in love with Resolute Bay at first sight. She was forever finding reasons to fly into the base.

Most of the flying was done in the old North Star aircraft. Those aircraft are now long gone and have never been missed by the passengers who endured long hours of eighty decibel torture while slung from the greasy, smelly, canvas seats. Not only was it inhumanly noisy – but the North Star was foodless in the early days. Although there was a small galley in the crew compartment, nothing but aromas ever escaped aft from its carefully guarded confines. The smells drove the passengers wild: coffee brewing, toast burning, soup bubbling, eggs and bacon frying. After six hours perched in the back of one of those monsters, tormented by the drift of heavenly scents, you were ready to strangle the crew one by one.

Not so our CBC correspondent. She managed, on each trip, to ingratiate herself with the captain and crew by volunteering to do the cooking for them. This arrangement pleased the engineer, who usually was joed for the job, and so our correspondent was welcomed "up front" as working crew. But the situation displeased any senior officers riding in the back, who were wont to say things about "that bloody woman civilian eating her head off, while we have to ride back here."

The woman became a character, widely-known throughout the service. On one trip she smuggled a cat into Resolute Bay. It was against all orders, but orders were not her long suit. This was the first cat ever to appear at this Arctic base, and the Eskimo families living nearby were fascinated with the strange, furry animal. The young CO, on the other hand, wasn't thrilled with the cat's presence; but he was afraid to challenge its female owner because of the power of the press.

Shortly after the North Star and its passengers departed, the CO found the cat using his shower stall for a lavatory. Enraged, he grabbed his service revolver and shot it. Then he carried it outside into the Arctic night and threw it on the garbage heap.

The next day, some Eskimos going past the base spotted the dead cat and took it home to their igloos. There the Eskimo women removed and tanned the pelt, and made it into two pairs of children's bedroom slippers. On his weekly visit to the Eskimo village the CO saw the slippers, and arranged to buy them. Returning to base, he hung them by a long thong over the bar (which was appropriately called the Polar Bar). They became a permanent conversation piece for visiting airmen.

When I returned to Montreal from a visit to Resolute Bay, the female correspondent telephoned me to ask about her cat.

"Did you see my cat when you were up north?"

"Yeah," I replied, not wanting to mention the cat's demise.

"Well?" she demanded. "What was it doing?"

"Oh," I said nonchalantly, "it was just hanging around the bar." Which seemed to please her.

*   *   *

The really fascinating thing about flying into Resolute Bay was the chance to visit the Eskimo settlement, which lay just a few miles south of the air base.

The government, as an experiment, had relocated five Eskimo families from the mainland of Canada to see if they could live in the high Arctic Islands. A Constable of the Royal Canadian Mounted Police, usually chosen for his ability to speak the Inuit language, was stationed at Resolute Bay to oversee the welfare of the natives. He kept strict control over visitors to the settlement, and no one was permitted to visit unless he acted as an escort.

One black January afternoon I went along with him in the big snowmobile when he was making one of his routine calls. The temperature was forty-five degrees below zero and the blackness of the day made it seem even colder. We had to use the headlights of the snowmobile to find our way over the frozen trail.

When we arrived at the first igloo, we had to get down on our hands and knees to crawl through the tunnel leading into the igloo itself. This was my first visit so I simply followed the Constable. Plodding along on hands and knees in the blackness of the tunnel my gloved hand landed on something furry just as a deep-throated snarl sounded in my ears. My heart stopped – but my legs and arms didn't, and I literally flew through the tunnel into the igloo. Once inside, I learned from the Constable that I had struck one of the huskies that slept in the tunnel. He thought my reaction was hilarious, but he didn't know how chicken I was around ferocious dogs.

When I had recovered from being attacked by a "wolf," I was introduced to a young Eskimo mother and her two children. They were all

dressed in furs and parkas and had the most beautiful black liquid eyes. Immediately, the lady of the house offered us tea. She poured from a kettle kept hot on a whale's jaw bone. The flame, supplied by seal oil, was hot enough to boil tea but not hot enough to raise the temperature and so melt the igloo.

While the Constable chatted away with the constantly smiling Eskimos I had a chance to look around the igloo. It was quite large, measuring perhaps twenty feet across and seven feet high at the centre, where a small vent was located. The family had covered the walls with pages torn from glossy magazines that the Constable had given them. This, I was told, prevented the walls from sweating and dripping water when the temperature in the igloo rose above the freezing point. The common bed was raised about two feet above the floor and was piled high with furs and skins.

Suddenly, the Eskimo woman put down her mug. Throwing on a parka and grabbing her heavy mitts she crawled rapidly into the tunnel. As the Constable prepared to go after her, I asked what was going on.

"She's going out to meet her husband," he said.

I hadn't heard a thing.

Now I was torn between wanting to see the husband's arrival and not wishing to challenge those lurking dogs. I gathered my courage and crawled swiftly through the tunnel, emerging just in time to see a swirling cloud of snow whirl up to us. An eight-dog team pulling a sled and driven by a fur-wrapped figure emerged from the blackness of the day.

The Eskimo who stepped off the back runners of the sled was smiling broadly. He said something to his wife and the Constable and disappeared into the tunnel. His wife was everywhere, unharnessing the dogs and tying them individually to stakes, pulling the sled around to the lee of the igloo, feeding a fish to each dog, and finally taking up the two white Arctic foxes her husband had caught. She knocked the powdery snow from the frozen foxes before she, too, crawled back into the tunnel.

Here we go again, I thought, and knelt down for the mad dash. When I entered the igloo once more the husband was sitting on the bed with a child on each knee. He had made tiny musical instruments from pieces of scrap wood and gut from animals. One was a very small violin while the other was a tiny guitar, and he pretended to play them as he sang to his delighted children.

As I stood there watching this marvellous scene I tried to compare it with what I knew existed in our large cities down south. I tried to imagine a man driving up to his home after work and throwing the car keys to his wife – telling her to park the car and unload the trunk while he strolled inside the house. And yet, in a sense, this Eskimo father had done just that after a day spent on the trackless, frozen wastes.

When I arrived back home in Montreal I told my wife how the Eskimos lived, and how the Eskimo wife cheerfully greeted her husband after her hard day's work. She wasn't impressed.

*   *   *

One of the more interesting jobs of Air Transport Command was the yearly resupply of the Arctic Islands weather stations. Four tiny weather stations were manned jointly by United States and Canadian personnel – civilians who were employed by the two weather bureaus. Four men from each country were stuck at each base for a year. Except for radio, their only contact during that time was the annual spring resupply operation of the RCAF.

Spring in the high Arctic came in April. Then the sun shone twenty-four hours a day, yet the ice was still thick and strong enough for heavy aircraft to land. The hub of the spring operation was Resolute Bay on Cornwallis Island. Ships brought the supplies from southern Canada to Resolute each summer, where they were stored for the next spring's airlift. Everything had to be airlifted at that time, so the pace was hectic and flying went on around the clock. Alert (on the tip of Ellesmere Island, about 400 miles from the North Pole) was one of the weather stations. Then, stretching southwestward on the edges of the islands, came Eureka, Mould Bay, and Isachsen.

Each weather base had three or four tiny wooden shacks, a radio tower, and miles and miles of miles and miles. The airfield was an ice strip, ploughed out on the sea ice as close to the camp as possible. Of course it melted in summer, and in winter it had no lighting. The only time a person could join or leave the camp was during the annual reprovisioning. The eight guys who had been locked in for a year were usually glad to see the first aircraft land.

There was one other touch of civilization that the camps experienced: the Christmas flights. Transport planes would make drops of special goodies and Christmas parcels and mail. Dropping the baskets could be tricky when the aiming point was only a tiny light in a sea of blackness. The panniers had to land close enough to be recovered, but not close enough to drop through the roofs. If they fell into the giant snowdrifts they could never be found.

One Christmas season the cook at Isachsen became ill, and it was imperative that he be airlifted out to hospital. A landing had never been made there in the darkness of winter – but after some rapid radio communications it was decided that one would be attempted if the camp could lay out a flare path on the ice. The weathermen made the flares from soup tins and oily rags, and the pinpoint flames were hardly visible from 1,000 feet. Bob Cook was the Captain of the North Star aircraft, and even though he had to approach the ice strip from behind a hill he made a really great landing. We were all glad to get down.

The late Frank Lowe, then a columnist with the *Montreal Star* and later editor of *Weekend Magazine*, was along on that flight. Since we had landed at Isachsen there was no need to drop the Christmas goodies, so we hand-carried some of them to the main hut. I remember that Frank was carrying a rope-wrapped Christmas tree. When he got into the hut he asked one of the weathermen where he should put it.

"What is it?" asked the guy.

"A Christmas tree," replied the astounded Lowe.

"Oh, throw it over in the corner someplace."

Frank and I decided that maybe a guy could get "bushed" living in such isolation. But it wasn't until Frank sat down in a chair next to the "library," an orange crate full of paperback books, that we were sure. The same weatherman sidled up to him.

"You're sitting in Jack's chair," he whispered.

*　　*　　*

In the 1950s, the RCAF followed the lead of the Americans and the British and formed a Ground Observer Corps across Canada. Thousands of civilian volunteers were asked to spot and report aircraft. Some manned observation towers and communications centres, while others worked in filter centres to plot the aircraft on large plotting tables. Still others, like housewives, kept their eyes and ears open and reported any sight or sound of an aircraft to their local organization. It was a vast network of very dedicated, unpaid citizens who eventually numbered in the tens of thousands. These were the days before powerful ground and airborne radar had been perfected, and Canada was most vulnerable to low flying aircraft.

The morale of the Ground Observers was continually reinforced by inspections and training visits from staff officers at Air Defence Headquarters. Lectures would be given in any old hall, basement, or other

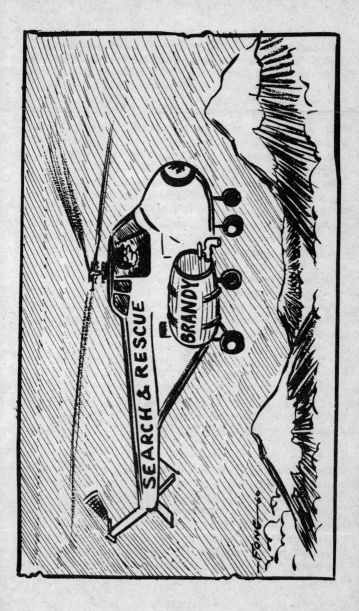

convenient location in hundreds of villages and hamlets across Canada. The cardinal point that was always drilled home was that radar was not infallible. Radar had its limitations – it could not see through or around a hill or mountain, and so was ineffective at low altitudes. This was where the civilian spotter could provide invaluable service by reporting any and all aircraft seen or heard.

Naturally, with so many enthusiastic novices involved, the odd mistake was made. Like the night in Quebec when a lumberjack snowshoed twenty miles through the bush to report the aircraft that had gone down on fire – and that turned out to be a falling star. Or the housewife who kept hearing a roaring engine noise as she washed her morning dishes. She reported an unseen aircraft, and when the local filter centre checked it out they found a bulldozer working away behind her home.

If the professionalism of the Ground Observer Corps occasionally fell a trifle short, the enthusiasm and gung ho public spirit of its members more than made up for any technical lapse. There was no doubt that it was a learning experience for the various RCAF staff officers assigned to guide the volunteers. Sometimes they tottered back to headquarters all bent and twisted.

At one memorable meeting in a church basement the question of why radar wasn't effective at low levels was expounded upon at great length. The point was always stressed to ensure that the spotters realized how valuable they were to the defence system. On this occasion, a lady in the front row raised her hand. She had a question.

"Did you say radar is no good at ground level?" she asked.

"Yes, ma'am, that's correct," replied the staff officer emphatically. "Radar is ineffective at low altitudes."

"Well, you're wrong. I got a ticket for speeding yesterday and the policeman said he used radar to catch me."

*   *   *

The Mid-Canada Radar Line stretched from coast to coast along the fifty-fifth parallel of latitude, passing through such exotic spots as Hopedale, Knob Lake, Great Whale River, Winisk, Bird, and Dawson. In reality it was an electronic fence. The theory was that an aircraft flying through its invisible beam would leave a signature. What Bell Telephone, Marconi, and the Defence Department hadn't thought about were the Canada Geese and other migrating species that flocked back and forth, setting off alarms. The radar line was only in use about ten

242

years before it was overtaken by more advanced radar systems.

Construction of the line was a staggering engineering feat; but it was so cloaked in defence secrecy at the time that its story was never fully documented by the press. While the main bases were in reasonably accessible locations, the small, unmanned, remote-control (remote) units were accessible only by helicopter. It was, in fact, the coming of age of the helicopter that permitted the Mid-Canada Line to be built. That region of Canada was so wild and rugged, the environment so hostile, that it could be built and maintained only by "choppers."

Cargoes were slung beneath the helicopters and lifted to tiny, remote detachments perched on the very peaks of high hills. Groundcrews had the lovely job of hooking and unhooking the cargo slings under the swirling blades of the choppers, surrounded by a maelstrom of blasting snow and ice. Temperatures of forty below zero were common in the winters, and the wind chill factor produced by the helicopters' whirling props created inhuman working conditions.

The remote camps were slaves of the main bases. Lights could be switched on, engines started, towers de-iced, and a host of electronic functions controlled from hundreds of miles away. All phone numbers were the same on each main site. If you rang 200 you got the CO on that base. If you added a prefix you got another CO at another site. All this was ready-made for the prankster. Late at night the local wit would dial every kitchen, coast to coast, and in authoritative tones tell the cook it was the CO speaking and would he please deliver a steak sandwich, pronto. Then he'd wait two or three minutes and phone again to give the cook a blast for taking so long.

Maintenance crews were flown into the remote sites on rotating schedules for overhauls or emergency repairs, and often weather would maroon them there for weeks. Well-stocked larders, and freezers overflowing with every type of delicacy gave some of the crews the long looked for opportunity to gorge themselves on their favourite food. One crew ate nothing but cream puffs for two weeks. Another ate steaks and nothing but steaks, morning, noon, and night. Yet another crew subsisted solely on canned fruit and frozen desserts.

The supply type who replenished the larders stumbled upon this freakish culinary pattern and reported his findings to the dieticians at Air Force Headquarters. Those energetic calorie counters tried their best to insist on balanced meals, but with little success. It was a guy's one chance in life to eat as much as he wanted of his favourite food – and no one within hundreds of miles to stop him.

The main Mid-Canada Line bases with airfields got more than their fair share of visitors, especially in the hunting and fishing seasons. Winisk, on the southeast corner of Hudson Bay, was a main stopping point for Canada Geese and Snow Geese on their annual migrations. They provided a great part of the food supply for the local Indians, who smoked and preserved the birds each fall, and hunting them with the Indians was a thrill often offered to visiting dignitaries. One who particularly enjoyed it was the Chief of the French Air Force, when he was on tour across Canada.

The French leader was fascinated by the Indians' ability to "talk" to the geese as they flew overhead, thus luring them in for a landing. For decoys, the Indians used whole wings from previous kills propped up in a well-chosen landing area close to their blinds, and as soon as the geese appeared overhead, the Indian Chief began talking or calling to them. When the birds got lower, and it looked as though they would come in for a landing, he changed his voice and the "talk" became more rapid. The geese seemed to answer him. When they put their feet and "flaps" down everyone stood up and blasted away with shot guns. The Indians tried to shoot the leader, which left the other geese in disarray. Those that escaped the first volley were called back and, amazingly, they returned to the calls of the Indians until all were killed.

That evening, there was a large dinner held for the French Air Force leader, and goose was a featured item on the menu. Everyone raved about the taste of the wild goose, and comments about its flavour, so much preferable to the tame taste of domestic goose, were passed around the table all evening.

The next morning, after the official party had departed, I was in the kitchen looking for someone when I happened upon a grocery bill. It was from a Winnipeg provisioner. I thought this strange because the usual practice was to buy food in carload lots, and the bills were handled by headquarters.

The bill I picked up was for a case of French wine, wild rice, and twelve geese.

*   *   *

Each Christmas season at Great Whale River (which is on the eastern shore of Hudson Bay, across from Winisk), the RCAF put on a large party for the Eskimo and Indian populations. The natives had built permanent settlements on the very edge of the Bay, and it was the most

244

southerly location in Canada for Eskimos. All ages took part in the out-door races and contests before attending the feed and dance indoors at the base. Even Santa Claus was included in the festivities.

It was during the snowshoe race over the river that I discovered the Eskimo wasn't a competitor. If he didn't have a chance of winning, he simply stopped running. When you asked him why, he would explain to you, very patiently, as though addressing a child, that it was obvious that he couldn't win the race – so why continue? There were no hard feelings. And it wasn't because they were sore losers, for they were constantly laughing and enjoying everything.

In the local one-room school, southern teachers would have a shock on the first day, when they found the centre row of seats empty. The Indian children sat on one side of the room and the Eskimo children on the other. They did this automatically, and so the teachers left them alone. The native village was similarly divided. The Indians lived in their huts on one side of the main street and the Eskimos lived on the other.

Many of these people were hired and trained to work on the Mid-Canada Line bases. They proved to be excellent workers, hardly bothered by the elements. It was a toss up who learned more from the situation – the natives, or the white folk from the south.

An order to an Eskimo was always taken literally. When the works foreman told an Eskimo snowplough operator to ''clean everything off the runway'' he got exactly what he had asked for. The control tower, of course, didn't appreciate having the lights ploughed away. Similarly, an order to the janitor to ''clean everything out of this hall'' resulted in the telephone being ripped from the wall and thrown out with the trash.

When the boiler house needed a couple of workers, two Eskimos were hired and trained to turn the various valves. Everything appeared to be going well until it was noticed that only one Eskimo was coming to work. He was working a double shift. When asked why, he said, ''No need for two.'' He had fired the other Eskimo. When it was explained to him that he couldn't be paid for both shifts, he brought the other Eskimo back.

Of course the Canadian government had already learned some valu-able lessons from our northern citizens. In the late 1940s, it had shipped four factory built houses to an Eskimo settlement to act as a trial replace-ment for igloos. When the crates arrived, the Eskimos built five houses.

*   *   *

One of the media types we frequently escorted to the Mid-Canada Line was a CBC person who had his own "Sportsman's Show" on television. Here he had background that wouldn't quit and an original cast of thousands. Indians and Eskimos, bush pilots and missionaries, Hudson Bay factors – not to mention the RCAF and civilian workers of the radar line. (And, incidentally, some of the world's best fishing and hunting.) As a side line, our personality did odd things like test outdoor equipment for various manufacturers in the "real" outdoors. Once, I escorted him on one of his movie making expeditions, and I learned how it was done.

We were to fly north in an old Dakota, and the Captain had hardly pressed the switches when a forty-ouncer bumped under my nose. It was about 0900 hours, a little early, I thought, for a libation. By the time we reached Winisk, though, I was certain that I was in close contact with the world's greatest outdoorsman. With the same charm he exhibited on his television show he told me tales of the rugged outdoors – of how with cunning and great skill he had outwitted the large trout, the giant moose, and the elusive deer.

When it came time to retire that evening I suggested to my charge that it would be an ideal night to test a new sleeping bag. The temperature sat at forty-five below zero. He agreed, and left to make the preparations while the rest of us got deeper into the card game.

In the morning, when I went looking for him, I found him snoring away in the sleeping bag – which he had placed on top of the bed!

"What the hell kind of test is that?" I wanted to know.

"Well," our outdoorsman sleepily replied, "I had the window open all night, so it's just the same as sleeping outside in the snow."

*   *   *

When a federal election hit the country back in the fifties, the "boys" at a Pinetree radar station decided one night, over the bar, to vote Communist.

There were only about a dozen officers on a Pinetree station so the event was hatched in relative secrecy. No one knew the Communist candidate, but they had read about him in the local weekly paper and decided that a vote for him might unnerve some people.

They were dead right. The votes had hardly been counted and announced nationally when all hell broke loose at National Defence Headquarters in Ottawa. Politicians were demanding to know about this

"Communist Cell" buried in the very heart of one of our most secret defence bases. What was going to be done about it?

The Minister of National Defence was demanding of the Chief of the Air Staff: "What is going to be done about it?"

The Chief of the Air Staff was demanding of the Air Officer Commanding, Air Defence Command: "What is going to be done about it?"

The Air Officer Commanding, Air Defence Command was demanding of the Commanding Officer of the radar base: "What is going to be done about it?"

The Commanding Officer suspected who his "Communists" were, but he was also calm enough to realize that a vote was a secret ballot, something all his superiors had forgotten in their wild panic. When this piece of enlightenment was passed back up the chain of command and laid on the politicians, they could only nod dumbly and try to act like they had never asked the question in the first place.

Meanwhile, the boys were toasting their scheme at the bar and calling each other "Comrade."

The Nature of Things

If there was one rule that was constantly pounded into our heads as navigator trainees at No. 5 Air Observer School, Winnipeg, it was: "Warn the pilot. Before and after taking celestial observations, warn the pilot." It was our request that he try and keep the aircraft straight and level for a period of three minutes, the time it took to complete one astro shot. Telling him when it was over allowed him to relax between the second and third shots. The consequences of failing to heed this rule follow.

It was one of my first night astro trips in an Anson in the late summer of 1944. The starry prairie sky was a navigator's dream, for hanging there like light bulbs were some of the brightest stars in the galaxy. We had only to choose and shoot. After dutifully warning the pilot each time, and completing a number of three-star fixes required by the exercise, I decided to take an extra. There would be no point in bothering the pilot, I thought. It would be buckshee, anyway. If he didn't keep the plane straight and level, what was the difference?

In the early Ansons, there were two ways to use the Mark IXA sextant – by shooting through the perspex dome in the roof of the aircraft, or by opening a side window in the passenger section, kneeling, and sticking your head out into the darkness. I chose the window. I might mention that because of the difficulty in manoeuvring while wearing the chest pack parachute, most navigators simply wore the harness and kept the chute within easy reach.

I pulled the window inward, propped it open, and knelt down, sextant in hand and the window ledge at about waist height. We were stooging along, nice and level, and my first shot on a star dead on our port beam was a beauty. The second, at about the eleven o'clock position, ditto. Now all I needed for a perfect, three-star-no-cocked-hat-fix was one at the seven o'clock position.

I shall never forget Altair.

Just as I pushed the trigger on the sextant to start the timer, the port wing dropped. There was obviously a fairly quick decision to be made here: let the sextant drop and use both hands to try to keep from falling out without a parachute – or join the sextant on the way down, thus avoiding a nasty board of inquiry.

I let the sextant drop, threw myself backward onto the floor, and lay there, shaking. My flying partner thought I was having a seizure and called the Captain, who decided he should radio base to have an ambulance meet us. I begged him not to, and explained what had happened.

"Well, let's see now," the pilot said. "You get seventy-five cents a day. At that rate it should take you two and a half years to pay for the sextant. But with your stupid disregard for the rules, you won't be around that long. If I were you I'd see the Sergeant over in stores. He may be able to save your ass."

I saw the Sergeant, who by some marvellous magic and devious shuffling of paper and forms, converted an unserviceable Astro Compass, one each, into a Mark IXA sextant, bubble. I often wonder, though, about the prairie farmer – trying to figure out how my heavenly contraption got buried in his south forty.

*　　*　　*

It was my first time on guard duty. This was at Edmonton in the dead of winter and brother, was it cold! I had to guard a long fence at the back of the camp where a rail line entered. We worked two hours on and four hours off, and the two hours in that sub zero cold seemed an eternity. I would run up and down the railway tracks trying to keep warm.

We had been taught how to challenge a person trying to enter the camp. I kept repeating such things as *Halt!* and *Who goes there?* and *Advance and be recognized!* as I tramped along in the cold. I had an old Ross rifle; but, of course, it was without ammunition.

I was cursing the cold and the air force when, to my horror, a train came along consisting of a locomotive and two box cars full of supplies for the station. It was then that I wished I had asked the Corporal what to do in such an emergency. But I was determined, just the same, not to let anyone or anything unauthorized into the camp.

"*Who goes there?*" I shouted to the engineer sitting up in the huge engine.

"Open the fucking gates," he replied.

"I can't let anyone in here without proper authority."

"Open those goddamned gates and hurry up!" he yelled.

"Just a moment while I blow my whistle," I said. And I started to blow my little tin whistle for help (even though it couldn't be heard over the noise of the train engine).

"Oh," said the engineer, "I can do that, too." And he began blowing his big steam whistle. He blew and he blew until everyone on the station was awake.

The guards came running – but not to my rescue. They relieved me of my duty.

*　　*　　*

252

There were many unsung heroes in the RCAF who did many difficult and dangerous jobs – jobs that, unless you were directly involved with them, would never cross your mind. The armourer was one person who had this type of responsible task, and his work was especially dangerous when it was associated with the bomb dumps. There, at the end of the airfield, hidden from view by trees or earthen barricades, the armourers worked away like so many moles. Day in and day out they loaded, fused, and transported monstrous-sized bombs – any one of which could blow up a station.

Given the nature and volume of the work there were, of course, accidents. Most were very explainable; but some, like the one in the story which follows, just seemed to happen ....

The scene was East Kirkby, April 17, 1945: a beautiful spring day with the end of the war in sight. The previous day, most of the aircraft had already been fitted with bombs – but now, at about 0930 hours, a change of load was called for. This caused a great deal of work. Much frantic preparation was needed before an early evening takeoff for the marshalling yards at Cham.

Many of the Lancasters were already fully loaded with 500- or 1,000-pound bombs; but the new requirement involved changing the fusing from "direct impact" to "long delay" on some thirty or more aircraft belonging to 57 and 630 squadrons. A large quantity of No. 53 chemical long delay pistols were required. We had to get some of them from a neighbouring base at Spilsby.

The bombs already loaded on many aircraft had to be taken off – either for a change of fusing or a return to the bomb dump. Normally, the change of fusing would be done in a fusing shed in the dump but, because of the large number of bomb trolleys which would be required, it was decided that a certain amount of the new fusing could be done at the aircraft dispersals. This decision added to the problems later on. It meant that some surplus bombs and detonators were still at dispersals awaiting return to the bomb dump when the explosion happened.

By about 1700 hours, work was still going on at 630 squadron, though the majority of its aircraft were bombed up and ready. At 57 squadron, preparations were complete. Planes were bombed up with a mixture of 500- and 1,000-pound bombs, all with No. 53 long delay pistols. Work was in hand to clear 57 squadron's dispersals of excess weapons, and the crews were due out to the aircraft between 1730 and 1800 hours ....

At 1740 hours, the first explosion took place. To the station armament officer, Flight Lieutenant John MacBean, it did not sound like a bomb. A photoflash maybe? At the moment he was on his way to tea, but he immediately turned back to base. Others were going the same way, although no one actually knew where the bang had come from. Had it been the bomb dump? But then, as MacBean headed down the perimeter track, he saw a cloud of black smoke over 57 squadron's dispersals.

Everything was in confusion. There was already considerable destruction just beyond the incendiary storage hangar, and people were rushing about. One badly burned armourer was lying near the hangar, his shirt gone. It had either been blown away or burned off.

MacBean quickly decided that it would be safer to approach the actual scene by going through the incendiary hangar. He knew only too well the fickleness of No. 53 chemical long delay pistols – they would not stand too much shock and heat. Just as he entered the hangar the fire tender arrived, and some of the firemen also made their way into the danger area.

The hangar contained some 300 tons of four pound and thirty pound incendiary bombs, the former made up of solid thermite (a form of magnesium alloy) the latter consisting of a methane/petrol mixture. The men found that the hangar's outer doors had been buckled and holed, and that one or two clusters of four pound incendiary bombs had been blown out of their stacks. They were already alight. If something was not done quickly, there would soon be a real conflagration!

MacBean remembered his own instruction to his staff: "Unless there is great danger to life and limb or vital property, don't try to extinguish any four pounders which function inadvertently." The reason for this instruction was that a certain percentage of the bombs were fitted with an explosive scatter charge. It was intended to discourage enemy firemen, and could be lethal at close range. This time, however, an attempt needed to be made.

MacBean ran back down the hangar to get a five gallon drum filled with sand. Then – just as he began to return – all hell was let loose. There was a tremendous explosion, which a corrugated hangar did nothing to lessen. MacBean found himself sitting on the floor while the roof above him shook under what sounded like a gigantic hailstorm. His cap was gone with the wind – and incendiary bombs, roller conveyors, and various other objects rolled and bumped on every side.

It was a wonder that they all missed him. But even more wonderful was the fact that the incendiary bombs were no longer alight. The blast of the explosion outside the hangar had extinguished the fires inside it.

* * *

We were scheduled to do a night drop for the army, and had loaded a three-quarter ton truck and a trailer aboard our C-130 aircraft. The drop zone was to be identified by a red light which an army reconnaissance ground team was to set up.

After a routine flight, the navigator signalled that we had reached the drop zone – but none of us could see a red light on the ground. I began an orbit and, after a while, there it was: a red light glowing in the darkness. I made one reconnaissance pass and then swung back to make the drop over the red glow.

It wasn't until we reached base that we were informed that the ground-crew had never made it to the rendezvous. The pickup truck had landed in a tree, while the trailer had gone right through the front porch of a farmer's house.

* * *

I was sent back to Canada after my first tour of operations to help sell war bonds. I must have been dragged to every cinema, church banquet, civic dinner, and factory lunch break in the country. Everywhere they could raise a crowd, there I was – living proof that one could actually survive a tour of ops and win a Distinguished Flying Cross as well.

I was taken, one evening, to St. Andrew's United Church in Sydney, Cape Breton. There I read the lesson, which I remember included every tongue-twister of a name in the Old Testament. Instead of giving a sermon, the minister sat aside so that I could provide a dissertation on what it was like flying over Germany. Just as the boys on my old squadron were doing "this very hour." (Wow, I thought, such drama.)

I began my little talk with an apology. Something to the effect that I felt like the remedy for a broken window. Instead of listening to the great words of their minister they had to listen to me. "I feel like some cardboard that one would put in a broken window. It's not the real thing – but it will have to do for one evening," I suggested.

After my talk, the minister escorted me to the back of the church to meet the congregation. One aged lady clasped my hand in both of hers and insisted that I was not at all like a piece of cardboard.

"You are a real pane!" she prayerfully alleged.

*   *   *

I was stationed at Centralia as a flying instructor when I decided to get married. The wedding was to take place in St. Lambert, just a few miles from RCAF Station St. Hubert, Quebec, on a Saturday in March. A group of fellow instructors decided that they would attend. Borrowing a C-45 Expeditor aircraft they would fly down for the festivities, taking turns at the controls so that they could get in some practice flying at the same time.

Saturday arrived – and so did the worst snow storm of the season. Nevertheless, the press-on types headed off for St. Hubert, and promptly got lost over the Adirondacks in New York State. They terrified themselves, and finally arrived late for the wedding, but the experience wasn't allowed to interfere with the celebrations that went on through the night, carrying across the river into Montreal. Most of the evening was spent disparaging the flying abilities of those whose turn it had been to be at the controls on the trip down.

When Sunday arrived it was bright and clear, a beautiful day for flying. Off they went back to Centralia, each with an excruciating hangover. This trip, however, the pilots who had suffered in the back seats the previous day had control. And they wanted revenge. They climbed the Expeditor to 10,000 feet and locked in the automatic pilot, setting it for a gradual descent. Then they "went to sleep."

Meanwhile, the pilots in the rear seats had gone to sleep as soon as they climbed aboard. All was smooth. The air was still and the small aircraft droned steadily on towards Centralia.

An hour went by before a stirring passenger looked out of the cabin windows and blearily realized that the aircraft was getting lower and lower. Concerned, he tried the cockpit door and found it locked. Looking through the window in the plywood door he saw two sleeping pilots, each slumped sideways in his seat. Jesus!

He began pounding on the door. When his fellow passengers awoke they, too, began pounding and yelling. Panic set in. Finally, one passenger grabbed the fire axe from its mounting and moved forward to chop

the door down. This was the signal for the ''sleeping'' pilots to awaken and have a revengeful laugh at their duped colleagues.

*   *   *

In wartime, you could expect to participate in a funeral parade on a fairly regular basis. One got used to being a pallbearer, or to being one of the honour guard or firing party. It was all a part of war.

Not so in peacetime military service, where deaths were, thankfully, not as common. A guy could go through his entire career without being chosen for a funeral parade. But, wartime or peacetime, they all had the same scenario – and I never was part of one that didn't threaten to burst every blood vessel, strain every sinew, and erode every ounce of composure I owned.

For the simple truth was that those funerals were funny. As we all know, tragedy and comedy lie just a hair's breadth apart, and the unintentional hilarity often caused by the participants in funeral dramas was magnified – like a joke in church – by the very solemnity of the occasion. Trying to maintain a military dignity while your insides were flying apart called for discipline of a very high order indeed. (I suspect that part of the reason ladies openly carry handkerchiefs at such affairs is because of their usefulness as gags. Crammed into the mouth at the appropriate time they successfully stifle screams of laughter – while providing an exhibition to other mourners of intense, heart-wrenching grief.)

So always, beneath the splendid detachment one assumed as a member of the honour guard paying collective last respects to an unknown comrade, a wonderful silliness took over. And it didn't require much to provoke secret mirth. There was the time the Group Captain lost his shoe in the graveside mud. Or the Montreal funeral parade for the late King George VI, when the bugle froze in the cold, reducing the Last Post to a sort of kazoo solo. But the occasion I remember best happened around 1954 in France, during the glorious early years of the RCAF's Air Division.

An officer had been killed in a motor accident near Paris. In the confusion that seized the integrated Allied force with which he served, some sort of international compromise was arrived at for the disposal of the remains. Normally, it would have been routine. But when the Americans, the Belgians, the British, the Dutch, and the French had all contributed suggestions, the body was embalmed (a rarity for France),

259

and duly deposited in a magnificent oak creation which had a lead lining – just as a final touch. Its empty weight was reputed to be 1,200 pounds. And the deceased had been a big man.

The cemetery was a beautiful place. At the end of a long, pea-stone path was a picturesque chapel, framed by tall lombardy poplars and swaying willows. The path had recently been replenished with stones, making it difficult to walk on – but the scene was an inspiration for our imaginative guard commander. He made good use of the time afforded by an overdue hearse to design a ceremony like no other.

Instead of the routine graveside service, he told us with excited enthusiasm, we, in the rifle party, would line the pea-stone path with rifles at the "present" as the casket was carried the 200 yards to the grave. We would fall in as it passed and follow it to the plot, where we would fire the traditional volleys in salute.

The first inkling of trouble was not long in coming. It began with a wheezing and whooshing sound. Out of the extreme corner of my curious eye, I discovered the source of the unusual noise: six flight sergeants, all overweight and degenerate from tax-free liquor and cigarettes, struggling with the heavy casket and the pea-stones. By the time the procession reached me, the red-cheeked pallbearers were gasping loudly. And then *karrunch!* The heavy casket nosed into the path.

Almost without hesitation, the six honorary pallbearers pitched in to help carry the load. This put six men on either side of the casket, each with a couple of fingers through the individual handles. It looked like a tall, staggering centipede as the valiant twelve struggled their way up the path. The close quarters forced upon them was complicated more than somewhat by the tendency of each bearer to remove the oxfords of the man in front of him.

When we all finally ground to a halt at the graveside, the panting sounded rather like the baying of twelve laryngitic bloodhounds. Fortunately, it drowned out the muffled snickers from those of us who wanted to leap into the bushes to unleash a well-justified shriek of laughter. Our mirth was intensified by the air of general concern when the enormous weight of the casket was set down atop the grave. The supports were two flimsy looking boards; and the congregation winced as they sagged deeper and deeper. By some miracle they held.

After the padre had said his part, it was our turn to salute the deceased with our gunfire. The command came. *Fire!* And out erupted a staccato roar, not unlike that of a string of large firecrackers. It took about five seconds before all the shots – which should have sounded as one – had been fired. Well, almost all the shots. In the stillness that followed, *bang!* went the last rifle. The paper wad that rendered the charge almost harmless hit an airman in the back of the head, twirling his wedge cap end-over-end across the cemetery. It spun him around on his heels to face us with a silly grin, his eyeballs counter-rotating in their sockets.

This was too much. Our stomachs and facial muscles knotted furiously, while the tremendous pressure of laugh suppression soaked our uniforms with perspiration. But we managed it. With some pride I can relate that we never did release that one fantastic laugh-out-loud that we needed so badly …. At least, not until we got into the truck that took us back to base!

*   *   *

In 1979, my wife and I were in England for a visit, and we decided to rent a car and drive up to St. Andrews in Scotland. When we got to Lincolnshire and the town of Boston old memories started flooding back – even though Boston wasn't the same as I remembered it. In fact, there was very little that was familiar. It seemed so busy and bustling compared to those days in the forties.

"Do you mind if I look for my old air force station?" I asked my wife hesitantly.

She smiled. "Go ahead."

"Well, I remember we used to drive out of town a bit. And then I think we turned up to the left somewhere …." I started to drive northwards out of Boston, and after a mile or two we did indeed come to a small road leading off to the left. "Let's just go up here," I said.

Sure enough, once on that small road we soon discovered a sign that said East Kirkby – and a little later, all that remained of the old station came into sight. Nothing was the same. It had been turned into a large farm, and the last hangar left standing was full of potatoes.

"I'd like to drive on the runway," I said quietly.

We drove up a narrow roadway onto the tarmac and looked at the remains of the once great takeoff runway. There were weeds growing through it. It was decaying, crumbling, and unusable.

"We took off for Berlin in the Lone Ranger one night on this very runway …. "

"Why did you call the plane the Lone Ranger?" my wife asked.

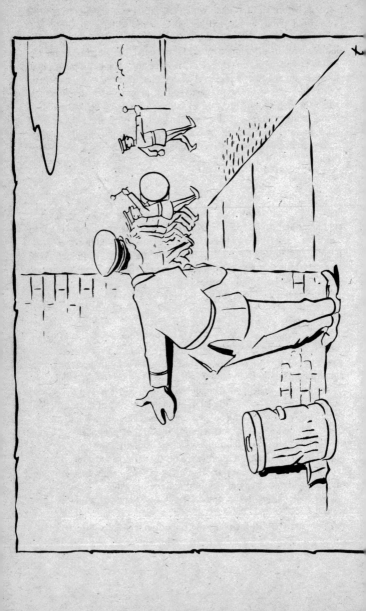

"I'll tell you some other time, but not now .... It sort of gives me the creeps – as if I shouldn't be around at all. It's just not the same." My hands tightened on the steering wheel. "Let's drive away from here."

We headed away from the airfield, and neither of us took a last look.

"I'm glad I saw it," I said. "But I'll never be coming back."